KICKING IT WITH THE WINGER

FOX ACADEMY

TL HAMILTON

FLUFFY FOX PUBLISHING

Kicking it with the winger

Copyright © 2023 by TL Hamilton

This book is a work of fiction. All names, characters, places, and incidents are the products of the author's imagination. Any resemblance to actual events, locales, or actual persons, living or dead, is entirely coincidental.

Cover Art © Stellar Graphics 2023

Editing: Heart Full of Reads

TL Hamilton

10 9 8 7 6 5 4 3 2 1

To you…

AUTHOR'S NOTE

Kicking it with the winger contains themes that may be triggering to some readers. Please use caution when reading.

Triggering themes include, but are not limited to:

Discussion of childhood trauma including SA

Alcoholism

Gaslighting (not between main couple)

Please exercise caution, and if you find yourself triggered by content, practice self-care whatever that may be for you.

# Chapter One

OSCAR

THE BODY beneath my shoulder hit the boards with a satisfying bump. The accompanying grunt made me grin into my mouthguard. Adrenaline coursed through my body. Fox fans drummed on the boards in appreciation as O'Leary shot down the ice unimpeded.

"You're a fucking pigeon," number forty-six growled, and I pushed away from him with a laugh.

"Keep chirping, just don't miss this next part." I winked and wheeled away, shredding the ice under my skates as I closed the distance between me and the biscuit O'Leary sent down the line.

The cool air of the rink kissed the small amount of exposed skin I had but did little to decrease the fire in my veins. Beneath my padding, my body was drenched in sweat. The clock ran down the final minutes, and while we were ahead, it was always dangerous to assume the game couldn't turn around in moments.

Like a well-trained pet, the biscuit slid neatly toward me, nestling into my stick.

"Beautiful," I muttered, leaning into my front leg. The wrist shot was a technique I'd been concentrating on perfecting since preseason, and as I followed through, I knew the puck would find goal. Holding my arms wide, I turned and sought out a red-faced forty-six as the lamp lit and the stadium exploded in sound.

"Fuck, yeah!" O'Leary screamed, thumping my shoulder as we sprinted for the bench, letting Foster and Cunningham hit the ice to run out the clock.

"I thought forty-six was going to throw hands for a minute there," O'Leary crowed, settling on the bench beside me and sliding his helmet off with a sigh. His dark hair stood out in all directions, slick with sweat. Reaching for a water bottle, I squirted the cooling liquid into my mouth before tipping my head back and half drowning myself with the rest of the bottle. After discarding my helmet, I wiped a sleeve over my face and grinned at my best hockey bro.

"He was just sore that he couldn't keep up with my mad skills."

O'Leary's chuckle was drowned out by the roar of the crowd as the final buzzer confirmed our winning streak continued. It was still early in the season, but we were off to a killer start.

The vibe in the locker room was next level as the guys joked and jockeyed with each other, buzzing with postgame adrenaline. The crack of a towel, followed by an unmanly shriek, made me chuckle as I slid out of my breezers. My undershirt was a sopping mess of sweat and I let it fall to the bench beside me with an unappealing splat as O'Leary slid in next to me.

"You coming out tonight, man? We're celebrating Foster's baby ass finally being old enough to drink."

Drinking on a school night probably wasn't the best idea, but it was a special occasion and hell if I'd be able to sleep while this adrenaline was pumping in my system. Grabbing my towel and body wash, I made a neat pile of my gear before answering O'Leary's questioning look.

"Yeah, I'll be there."

But first…it was time for a well-earned shower.

***

"You smell amazing," the puck bunny beside me shouted in my ear as she leaned in and buried her nose in my collarbone. "Although I bet you smell better straight after a game. All sweaty and dirty…" She let the implication of what else would make us sweaty and dirty hang as she pressed her chest into my shoulder. She was cute. Long blonde hair pulled back in a long tail that any man could imagine wrapping around his fist.

Unfortunately for her, I knew damn well she'd spent the night wrapped in Foster's fist just last week and as much as some of the boys were happy to assist the bunnies' life goals of bagging the entire team, I wasn't interested in being anyone's trophy.

Katie, or Kylie, or whatever her name was, leaned in again as the lights dimmed and a disembodied voice welcomed us to Madame Cognac's Sparkle and Seduction burlesque night.

We sat in plastic chairs arranged in a loose semi-circle around a large corner of the room where blocks and screens were set up, ready for the show. As the voice finished its introduction, a spotlight flicked on behind a large white screen, silhouetting a female body that looked to be covered in feathers. I shuddered, thinking of the birds, those things could have come off, and ... Kirsty?...took it as an invitation to sidle even closer. She was practically in my lap by this point, but at least she wasn't wearing feathers. Music played over the speakers, and I noticed several of the boys straighten from the corner of my eye as the female began to dance.

"Ugh, what an attention whore," Kandy huffed. Karlie? What was her name? I knew it started with a K, but hell if I knew what the rest was. I was usually pretty good with names, too.

Politely keeping to myself that she was acting rather desperate for attention herself, I turned my attention back to the show as the woman stepped out from behind the screen. Yup. She was covered in feathers. My skin crawled at the sight.

"Anyone need a refill?" I asked, disturbing my companion as I hightailed it to the bar like a bitch to escape the byproduct of the most evil creature in existence.

I managed to miss the rest of the performance waiting for a round of beers and returned to my seat to find a distinct lack of feathers on the stage. It was a shame the same couldn't be said for my eager seatmate.

"You're back," she said, bouncing out of her seat and almost upending the tray I had balanced on my hand.

Players started reaching for drinks, and I snagged my own bottle before I missed out.

"Thanks Cav-man," Cunningham said, taking the last beer and the tray off my hands.

"All good, my friend, just don't have too many. Coach will kick all our asses if anyone's hungover tomorrow."

"True that." Cunningham saluted me with the bottle before he tipped it up and downed half the bottle. As he took a breath, the light glinted off the labret piercing he'd put back in after the game.

The MC finished her banter and announced the next act as I settled back into my seat, praying for lace or sequins instead of more feathers.

A roll of bongos, then horns, started playing, and I recognized "Cuban Pete" from watching *The Mask* as a kid. My mom was a huge Jim Carey fan, and I knew most of his movies, word for word. I grinned in anticipation, knowing anyone who chose this particular song had to have a good sense of humor.

"Wouldn't you rather go somewhere quieter? You could show me why they call you Caveman." Khloe let the invitation hang, but before I could answer, a tall, dark-haired vixen ran onstage, covered in balloons. She pranced around the open floor, teasing and twirling, and came up with a long black cigarette holder. Stopping in the center of the stage, she popped two balloons and revealed a tantalizing glimpse of the olive skin on her side. The room went nuts as she shimmied over to Foster, gave him the cigarette holder, and pointed to a balloon to pop. Foster's face flamed a darker red than his hair, but he followed instruction and grinned as he handed back the cigarette holder. The performance was geared toward fun. Where others had been overtly sexual, this girl wanted to play and have the audience play right along with her. I was entranced. Through audience contribution and her own popping, her curves were uncovered one pop at a time, and I found myself on the edge of my seat waiting for each new piece of skin to be unveiled.

As the balloons dwindled, she danced toward our corner again and presented her popping stick to Karen, who flopped back in her seat with a huff. This girl didn't seem to like anyone she thought was competition. Without missing a beat, Balloon Girl held the stick out to me instead. Meeting her silver eyes, I popped the balloon over her thong-covered ass and handed her stick back with a smile. I could have sworn she gave me a genuine smile back before she shimmied off to finish the routine.

By the time she finished, she wore nothing but a thong and little tassel things over her nipples and a small part of me wanted to punch all my teammates for the way they hooted and hollered as she left the stage.

As the next act walked out with a huge feather fan, I decided it was time for a bathroom break, so avoiding eye contact with Klara lest she get any ideas, I slipped into the dimness of the rest of the room. Spotting Fordham on the way back from the bar, I lifted my chin in greeting and received one in return.

"*I'll save you one,*" he mouthed, lifting the tray in his hands. Good man. The whole team had needed this night of decompression. Our training schedule had been insane during the preseason, but now that the season had started and we were on a winning streak, Coach didn't want to change anything in case it ruined our luck. Which meant we were all exhausted between starting classes for the year and training.

Ducking down the hall with a large sign pointing out the restrooms, I found myself humming "Cuban Pete" as I put the urinal to good use and washed my hands. Damn, that dancer had been something. She looked about my age, and I wondered if she went to Fox Academy. Nah, surely I would have noticed her around. With images of the dancer fresh in my mind, I pushed through the restroom door and noticed two shadows at the far end of the corridor. One was tall and masculine, the other maybe a head shorter and curvy. The song in the main area ended, giving me a snippet of the argument that was unfolding in the dark corner.

"You can fuck right off, Brady. I don't have time for this." Her voice was deep and smooth. Confident. I liked that she didn't seem intimidated by this dude whose size was close to mine.

"You're going to make time for me. I came a long way to see you. I refuse to let you shut me out." The male figure stepped in toward the female, and she shifted. The light from the exit sign fell over her face, and from where I stood, I made out the features of Balloon Girl.

My body lurched in an unconscious step toward her, but before I could do more, she pushed through the exit, and left 'Brady' standing there with his metaphorical dick in his hand.

"There you are, man. Mandy's looking everywhere for you." Foster stumbled into me with a sloppy hug.

"Who?" I asked, tearing my gaze from the door where, I'd just realized, Balloon Girl had chosen to walk out into late November weather in nothing more than a thong. Foster pointed across the room at the bunny whose name I'd gotten terribly wrong. Mandy did not start with a K. *Oh well.* Balloon Girl's harasser chose that moment to shoulder past Foster and me, the asshole too busy muttering to himself to apologize for knocking Foster aside. As Foster nattered on about the show and how badly Mandy apparently wanted me, half my mind was calculating how many hours we had until practice and whether Foster would be sober for it.

The other half was still on Balloon Girl.

Chapter Two

MIA

My ALARM PULLED me from sleep far too early for my liking the next morning. I reached for it blindly, pushing snooze, and settling back down for a little bit more oblivion before I had to start the day.

"You really shouldn't do that," my roommate, Violet, warned as she gathered her books and shoved them into her Fox Academy backpack.

"Why?" I groaned, cracking one eye to glare at her from my nest of pillows and bedspread. It had taken me hours to warm up when I got home from the club the night before.

I'd walk out half naked again if it meant avoiding a conversation with Brady, but the walk around the building had been hella brisk.

"Because that's the fifth time you've pressed snooze and I'm about to head to class. You're going to be late and you're still sparkly."

I looked down at the mess of sequins and glitter that covered my usually white bedspread.

"Shit."

Glancing at the clock, I cursed again and forced myself out of bed. Huh. I was still wearing the thong and tassel pasties from the night before.

Violet rolled her eyes with a smirk, used to my casual nudity around our dorm room at this point. "What subject have you got this morning?" I asked.

Her groan gave me my answer, even before she told me she was headed to math class. Carefully peeling my pasties off, I threw a robe over my shoulders and grabbed my shower caddy.

"Just think. Every class is a class you'll never have to take again," I assured her as I ran out the door and down the hall to take the fastest shower of my life. Did I have time for it? No. Was there a chance in hell I'd go to class smelling of sweat and looking like a five-year-old's craft corner? Also no.

Ten minutes later, I was back in my room, throwing clothes out of my closet in search of something clean and pulling my wet hair into a messy bun. With my cell and backpack in hand, I sprinted across campus and into the Pearl Building. Shit. I really didn't want to be late for this class. I needed to pass it, and pissing off the teacher this early in the semester didn't seem like a good precedent to set. Without slowing my pace, I hurtled around the last corner and collided with an immovable mass outside the door of my classroom. The force of the impact made me reel, and I would have landed on my ass if a strong hand hadn't whipped out and steadied me on my feet. The contact was too unexpected. Too large. My mind screamed threat, and

I almost fell a second time while pulling away from the grip.

"Hey, hey. I'm sorry. Are you all right?" His voice was deep and soothing. I didn't like it. I'd learned early in life that if something seemed safe, it was probably just good at hiding the danger. Pulling my confidence around me like a blanket, I straightened my spine and looked up — way up because this dude was tall, even for me — into an eerily familiar face. Dark sandy blond hair flopped into green eyes that looked through me the same way they had the night before at my show. His nose was warped in a way that hinted at having been broken at some time in the past, but the freckles dusting over his pale skin kept him looking mischievous rather than thuggish. Long, thick lashes pressed together as his expression changed from concern to recognition.

"I know you."

"No, I think you have me mistaken for someone else." I'd had a couple of schoolmates recognize me in the past, and it hadn't always gone well. Some people assumed that because they had seen your body, they had a right to it. I was always quick to disavow them of any such notion.

"No, I do. I saw you last night. I was worried when I saw you head outside after your set," he said. Curiously, as he spoke, he took a half step back and leaned against the wall on the opposite side of the door, arms crossed over his wide chest. He was offering me an out if I wanted it.

"Just went out to cool off a little." I shrugged it off, hoping he hadn't seen too much of the confrontation. Damn Brady, coming in and messing with my life again. He was supposed to be my past. I wanted him to stay that way.

"I'm Oscar," he offered, still making no move to invade my personal space.

Ten points to Oscar for showing some respect.

I glanced at my phone, about to introduce myself in turn when the time caught my eye.

"I'm… Shit, really late." With a panicked look at my new friend, I pushed through the classroom door and froze in front of a sea of eyes.

"Miss Maddren, Mr. Cavanaugh, nice of you to join us. Please take your seats and do not disturb my class further." Mrs. Murdoch's voice sounded pleasant, but I knew from experience she was not the teacher to cross. Hustling to my seat in the back corner, I pulled out my sports psychology textbook and resolutely ignored Oscar's eyes as he did the same. I hadn't noticed him in class before. Not that I paid much attention to others, because my degree was important and I needed to spend my class time learning so I could spend any spare time I had earning a wage to pay for my tuition. My brother, Luca, contributed what he could, but he had to support himself too. Being on the national swim team didn't start paying well until they had the chance to start bringing home medals. Plus, Luca had done enough over the years. We'd survived to adulthood because we were resourceful and good at supporting each other. My pride wouldn't let him take on all the financial burden now.

"Miss Maddren?" Mrs. Murdoch looked at me expectantly.

"Mental toughness, motivation, goal setting, anxiety and arousal, and confidence," a deep, now familiar voice, said loudly.

"The five theories of sports psychology we'll be exploring. Sorry, Mrs. Murdoch, was that question not for me? I zoned out for a minute there." From where I sat, I could see his apologetic expression in profile and it looked almost genuine until Mrs. Murdoch turned her back with a huff and Oscar shot me a conspiratorial wink across the room. I smiled in thanks and focused on the rest of the lesson so I wouldn't be caught out again.

Sixty long minutes later, our class was let out, and I hurried to follow a tall, scruffy brown head out of the building.

"Thank you," I panted, catching him just as he started across the parking lot. I couldn't believe how long his legs were. I was five foot ten and the only person I knew who was a struggle to keep up with was my brother, but that was because he was a freaking giant.

At the sound of my voice, Oscar turned, already smiling.

"Happy to help. You seemed like you were a bit in your own head," he said, waiting until I was beside him before continuing to walk but at a slower pace than before.

"Ahh, yeah. I was… distracted."

Oscar grunted, tucking his hands into the pockets of his sweats and we walked for a while in silence.

He was doing it again. Making me feel all comfortable with him. I wasn't sure why I was even still walking with him. Or where we were going. We made it to the other side of the parking lot and crossed the front of the high school dorms before turning right between the dorms and the ball field. He steered us toward the skating rink, and it hit me like a freight train. Those had been hockey players at the show. He must be part of the team.

The realization sunk in that I was in the presence of Fox U's current sporting royalty. He took a deep breath, and I braced for whatever he was about to want from me.

Here we go. No more nice guy. At least now I'll know his agenda and I can get on with my day.

"I have to ask," he said, slowing to a stop at the door of the rink.

I raised a brow at him, unwilling to give him anything, but also unable to stop myself from wrapping my arms around my waist.

"What made you use "Cuban Pete" for your performance? Isn't it a little outdated for you?"

I opened my mouth. Closed it. Tried desperately to find the thread of the conversation that led back to my choice of song.

"Like… was it a rhythm choice? Did someone older teach you the dance? It's just… not many people our age would even know that song, let alone choose to perform to it." He cursed, slapping himself on the forehead. "Sorry, that came out wrong. I'm just wondering how someone like you knows that song."

He rubbed the back of his head in a way I was trying not to find adorable as he backpedaled.

Wait. No. I didn't find it adorable. Not at all.

"My brother had *The Mask* on VHS. He used to play it for me when I was growing up." I didn't mention it was often a distraction for me after I'd taken a beating from one of our mom's boyfriends, or worse, when Luca was about to take one for me.

Our upbringing wasn't something I ever wanted to talk about, but some days lying there, watching the tape that was so worn that parts were discolored, and pretending I was Tina Carlyle was all that got me through to the next morning. The day that video tape broke, I sobbed for an hour.

"That's cool," Oscar said, breaking through those intrusive thoughts. "My mom is a huge Jim Carey fanatic so I grew up on his movies. *The Mask* was one of my favorites. So now I know you have a brother, but I still don't know your first name, Miss Maddren." He smirked, clearly thinking of how displeased Mrs. Murdoch had been with us earlier.

There was no part of the interaction that I should have encouraged. I had enough going on in my life and none of it included letting a jock get close enough to hurt me. So, it made no sense when I opened my mouth and out poured my name.

"Mia, huh? That's much prettier than Balloon Girl," he said.

"What…?"

"Oh." He chuckled self-consciously. "That's what I was calling you in my head. You know… because of the balloons…"

"Makes sense," I agreed, trying to keep the corner of my mouth from ticking up into a smile.

"I… Yeah. So, anyway. Mia. Could I maybe ask if you'd like to grab a coffee sometime?" The cutest pink flush crept up his neck and I wondered how a jock, who clearly had girls throwing themselves at him — yes, I'd seen the one hanging off him the night before — could be so nervous asking out someone like me.

Alarm bells rattled in my head and I realized I wanted to say yes to him. Coffee meant talking. Talking meant vulnerability. So not my scene.

"You know, the football team is having a house party tomorrow night. Maybe I'll see you there?" I offered, trying to keep my voice neutral.

Oscar blinked. "Yeah, definitely. I'll, uh, I'll see you there, then."

I pretended not to see the look of disappointment on his face as he headed into practice.

God, I was such a bitch. Why couldn't I be normal?

I knew the answer, even if I didn't like it. I would never be normal. The nicest thing I could do for Oscar was to leave him alone. Let him find a nice girl to go to all his games and wear his jersey. Settle down and have two point five children and live mortgage free because his professional career paid his house off in his first season. Retire at forty before his injuries force retirement on him and go into a sports journalism career. I wondered what he was studying. Then I wondered why the hell I was standing outside the hockey rink, planning out the life of a guy I just met so I could ensure I wasn't in it.

Fuck.

I was losing my mind.

Again.

Chapter Three

OSCAR

THE MUSIC WAS PUMPING, and the two-story house already at capacity when I wandered into the party with a six-pack of beer I had no intention of finishing. My mom had drilled it into me that bringing your own drinks was part of being a good houseguest, so despite this being a kegger where others would be writing themselves off, I'd stick to two beers and be relatively fresh for training come morning.

This plan was going to work. Maybe if things went well, I could convince Mia to come and hang out by one of the outside heaters so we could actually talk and get to know each other. Weaving my way through the crowd, I found enough room in the fridge to wedge five of my beers and leaned back against the kitchen counter to watch a line of juniors throw back tequila suicides. My eyes burned just watching them snort the salt, but only one of them dropped out before the lime juice-in-the-eye conclusion to the stupid game. Shaking my head, I sipped my beer and strolled into the living room to see who else was around because I was friendly like that. Definitely not because if I could convince Fraser to give up his seat, then I'd have a prime view of the front door. Which Mia would definitely need to come through when she arrived.

Nah. Nothing like that.

Beating some redhead out for the couch arm next to Fraser, I stretched myself out along the back of the seat and started playing with his hair, ignoring the glare he sent me for the neat cock-block move I'd just pulled. Twirling his rust-colored strands into spikes, I suppressed a chuckle as he tried to continue his conversation with one of the wide receivers while batting at my hand periodically. As though I were a fly that would buzz off if shooed hard enough. Not likely.

He lasted longer than expected, finishing the red cup in his hand before he finally blew his top.

"For fuck's sake, Cav-man. Will you please leave me alone? What do you want?"

"What do any of us want? To play hockey, find the love of a good woman, a nice place to sit our ass down and watch the world go by…"

"Jesus Christ, you're not even drunk. Are you? Fine. I need another beer, anyway. This way, I can go find the bunny your stupid ass chased off."

I chuckled, sliding into the seat as he stomped away.

"You know that was an asshole move, right?" the receiver — his name might have been Mike — said with a grin.

"Not my fault he isn't comfortable in his sexuality," I said with a shrug, taking a long pull on my beer. My seatmate chuckled, saluting me with his own bottle.

"So you're the shit-stirrer of the hockey team, huh? We got one of those." He pointed toward a group of guys gathered around a beer-pong table. The group let out a roar of approval as someone cursed up a storm on the opposite side.

"Nah, I just know what I want," I said, perking up at a disturbance near the door.

"Mads!" Liam Anders, captain of the swim team, yelled, crossing the room and sweeping a woman not much shorter than him into a hug. Long, dark brown hair swung wide as they did a half spin, and I was out of my seat before I remembered I was supposed to be playing it cool.

She playfully slapped him on the chest and pecked a kiss on his cheek, and I saw red until she pushed away from him and greeted the next person in line. I took a deep breath and pulled my emotions back into line through pure will. It didn't hurt that the guy immediately turned and disappeared into the crowd, and I'd checked where his hands were on her. It looked platonic, but I was willing to reassess if he got near her again.

"She's something, all right," Mike said, eyeing Mia as she hugged a tiny blonde woman hello.

"She's spoken for," I said without blinking.

"Oh, sorry man, I didn't know." He backed away, hands up in surrender, and I became aware my fists were clenched and I'd angled my body between him and Mia. Even if she didn't know it.

Even if she wasn't mine.

Hell, it looked like I was living up to my nickname when it came to this woman.

Over the music, I could have sworn I heard the tinkle of laughter, and I looked back to see her grinning at the tiny woman in front of her.

Ok, I'd given her long enough. Now it was my turn. All but pushing through the residual crowd waiting to greet the goddess in their midst, I leaned in close enough to speak in her ear.

"Fancy meeting you here, Balloon Girl." The hair at the nape of her neck rose as she turned toward me.

I wasn't ready for the full force of those silver eyes. Somehow, they'd dimmed in my memory over the intervening hours since I'd left her outside the rink.

There was a problem, though. The smile on her face was as fake as my mom's pleather sofa.

"How are you, Oscar?" she asked, pushing up on her toes to peck a kiss on my cheek. "Are you having a good night?"

"I am now that you're here." I tried to rally, even as my brain was screaming something wasn't right.

"That's sweet. I think I'm going to get a drink. Do you need one?" She glanced at my half-full bottle and turned toward the kitchen.

What the fuck just happened?

I played back over our conversation the day before. Okay, fine, I hadn't been in stellar form, but I also didn't think I'd done anything to warrant fake smiles and distant kisses. As though a leash had pulled tight, I wandered listlessly after her, trying to develop a plan to get back on track.

While I didn't sleep around a lot, I had no problem with women. Not to brag, but I could usually have anyone I wanted. Except, apparently, the only one I was interested in.

Maybe I was just too much in my own head. As Mia retrieved one of my beers, I focused on getting back in the game.

"Tell me, Balloon Girl, do you have skills?" I asked, leaning against the counter and watching as she twisted off the top and took a long pull.

"I think you saw my skills last night, Gretzky."

Fuck, that was hot.

If she kept using hockey references, I'd be putty in her hands forever.

I just had to educate her on one thing.

"Nice try, but the great one was a center."

She mirrored my pose on the island, so we were almost toe to toe.

"Oh, my apologies." She gave me an exaggerated pout. "So what position do you play, then? Enlighten me, O God of the ice."

"I'm a winger. The rest you got right, though. I quite like the thought of you calling me God."

Her throat worked for a moment before she raised her bottle and took another long draw.

So I did have an effect on her. Hell yeah.

Unsure how much longer I could keep my cool, I took her hand and led her toward the designated beer pong table.

"These are the skills I was asking about," I told her, intentionally keeping her hand in mine as we watched two of my teammates go head-to-head in a last-cup decider.

Glancing down at her, I got caught in her stare. Those silver eyes twinkled in challenge, and I found I couldn't look away, even as the crowd roared and moved in around us to congratulate the winner. Behind the playful look, a shadow moved. The same shadow I'd noticed when I saw her perform. It called to me like a siren's song, a tune I'd heard before and one I was determined to uncover before it was too late. I'd failed someone with that shadow before, and I was realizing that I couldn't make the same mistake again.

"I never back down from a challenge," Mia said, pulling me toward the table with a grin that broke me out of my morose thoughts.

Slapping a smirk on my face, I forced myself to check back into the moment, squeezing her hand before I moved away from her to the other end of the table.

"Bring it, Maddren," I said over the cheers and catcalls of our peers.

Once our beers were racked, we used eyes to decide on playing order. Maintaining eye contact with her, I made a shot at her cups and missed. I shot an 'aw shucks' look at Mia as my ball caught the edge of the table and shot into the crowd. Over the noise of the room, I could have sworn I heard her chuckle. Deep, melodic, and so damn sexy my dick sat up and took notice. Without batting an eye, she answered my poor shot with a perfectly placed ball in my center cup. Immediately, buzz started up around the table of beginner's luck as a dark-haired senior student handed Mia three balls so she could take the first turn. Hell, most of the team would have agreed, but I had a sneaking suspicion I was being hustled. Her first two shots fell neatly into two cups in the third row of my triangle, and I downed them as her third shot went wide. I took my first three shots and nailed all of them, smirking at her as she rolled the balls back. My next shot went wide, and I waited while she drank her own cups. "Stop holding back, Balloon Girl. Show me what you got," I taunted, spreading my hands to showcase my four remaining cups. Four shots and I was out. Her aim was impeccable, the look of triumph on her face hot as fuck as she bowed out of the next game and circled the table to commiserate with me on my loss.

"You're a shark, aren't you?" I teased, wrapping an arm around her and guiding us toward the back patio where several heaters had been set up to keep the overflow party attendees warm.

"Only at beer pong," she said with a shrug. "I don't know my way around a pool table to save myself. It's a niche skill with very little transferable application." I laughed at her attempt at humility and steered us toward a quiet corner at the edge of the pool of light.

"So, what other secrets are you keeping?" I joked, settling my ass on the low brick wall that ringed the patio. Mia froze, her whole body going still, and I cursed myself. I knew there was something there, but it didn't mean I had the right to demand it of her on the first date. Trust was critical, and not something that could be fast tracked.

"Well, you know I'm a hell of a dancer," she muttered, stepping into the space between my knees.

"I do know that," I agreed. Her hands took a long slide up my thighs as she stepped closer, tilting her head to the side as she eyed my lips.

"That's one highly transferable skill. Care to find out?" My dick throbbed in agreement as she reached up and sealed her mouth over mine. She tasted like beer and cherries, an intoxicating combination that I couldn't get enough of. I took over the kiss, licking my way into her mouth and twisting a hand into her hair. I loved how she fit against me. Hauling her closer, I tilted her head back for a better angle and devoured her like my last meal. Deep noises of pleasure rumbled out of her throat as her hands roamed under my shirt, nails scraping over my chest and abs, causing me to shudder. The clink of metal pulled me from the fog of lust that had settled over my brain and, struggling hard to focus, I noticed my belt was unbuckled.

"Mia."

"It's ok, no one can see. Just relax."

"No, wait."

My dick screamed at me to shut the fuck up, but something wasn't right here. I didn't want Mia for a quick lay, and it seemed like she was shutting me out, even as her hand slipped past my waistband. As gently as I could, I put her away from me and refastened my belt.

Mia's eyes narrowed dangerously.

"What's wrong? Is Mr. Bunny Boner not interested in a dancer? Would you rather me hang off your teammates for a little while first?" My vision flashed red at the mention of my team. No. None of them would be allowed anywhere near her. Shoving down the possessive impulse, I addressed the other implication she'd thrown at me.

"Trust me, my reputation is unfounded. I just think people should get to know each other before —"

"They see each other's parts? I guess there's no value in mine because you've already seen them, right? No challenge? Fuck you."

"No! I —"

Mia darted through the back door and disappeared into the crowd.

"I'd love to see your parts," I yelled as the song ended. The entire room erupted in cheers and several people lifted their shirts to show me their *parts*. I let the chaos flow around me as I desperately searched for a glimpse of long, dark hair or silver eyes.

She was gone.

# Chapter Four

Mia

WHAT THE HELL was wrong with me?!

I threw myself at him because he playfully hinted I had a secret? No wonder he didn't want me.

Old Mia weaponized sex. New Mia was supposed to know better.

Logically, I knew Oscar wasn't a threat to me, but there were parts of me I desperately wanted to keep hidden, and every time he looked at me, it felt like he *saw* me.

I didn't like how much I wanted to be seen. By him.

A shiver worked its way up my spine and I pulled my coat tighter around my body, unwilling to leave my perch just yet.

After Oscar mortifyingly — yet totally understandably — rejected me, I fled the party and came to my favorite thinking spot. Hell, maybe New Mia was around. Old Mia would have found the nearest willing body and fucked them loudly in a public place until she'd blown up any chance of Oscar speaking to her again.

So… progress.

I released a heavy breath and watched the cloud of steam dissipate slowly in the chilled air. On a whim, I formed an O with my mouth and tried to blow smoke rings the way Luca and I had when we were young. Standing at our school bus stop, rarely dressed for the cold weather, we'd pull sticks from nearby trees and puff on them as though we were high-class socialites like we saw on TV.

Just like it did back then, my breath refused to be shaped and looked more like a steam train tackling a hill than any kind of fancy rings.

From up here, I could see all of Fox Academy, both the college and the high school side of the campus, and in the distance, Oak Hills. The stadium lights were still on in the baseball stadium, and I imagined the poor cleaners wandering around in this cold, silently cursing out the spillers of beer and popcorn as they swept out the stands after this afternoon's game. I wasn't sure who had won. Maybe if I'd stayed a little longer at the party, I would have found out.

I swung my feet idly, uncaring about the four-floor drop beneath them. In junior year, I discovered that the female dorm had roof access and that no one else seemed to see the attraction in frequenting the area. A waist-high brick wall was the only safety feature to keep over-stressed underachievers from seeing if they could fly. I shook my head, forcing out the intrusive thought as I turned my attention back to the view.

I needed to get back into yoga. When I wasn't grounded, my mind ran a million miles per hour in every direction. The earlier scene with Oscar wasn't helping my state of mind, either. The ostrich was my spirit animal, and if I had any say in it, I'd do my damndest to never have to face Oscar again. If he didn't see me, he couldn't hurt me. And if my mind's refusal to let go of the evening's events was any indication, he already had the ability to do more than hurt me. He could completely destroy me.

A vibrating in my pocket jolted me out of the depressing realization.

"What...?" Retrieving my cell, I stared blankly at the caller ID, *The Devil*. Why wouldn't he leave me alone?

Rejecting the call, I cocked my hip to slide the phone away, but it immediately started vibrating in my hand.

"Don't do it, Mia."

I knew Brady wanted to have a conversation. I'd run out into the freezing cold to avoid it the night before. He was my past, and nothing he could say would change that.

I rejected the call again and swung my legs back over the brick railing. I didn't want to associate Brady with my quiet place, and I'd been watching the pavement. Oscar hadn't followed me back to the dorms.

Good. I was happy about it. Really, I was.

He'd caught a glimpse of Mia in survival mode and run the other way. It was for the best.

And denial wasn't just a river in Egypt.

I jogged down two flights of stairs and cursed loudly as my cell buzzed again.

A leggy blonde gave me a once-over that was steeped in judgment as she strode past me. I had two choices.

I could turn my cell off, crawl into bed, and hide from the world until I had to go to work at seven AM, or I could be an adult and find out what he wanted.

The buzzing ceased as I dug out the keys to my dorm room and resumed before I'd turned the key in the lock.

With absolutely zero regrets, I sent a text out to Violet telling her I was home and would be unreachable and powered down my cell.

The desk drawer was where Violet and I kept our candy stash. We were fairly certain we had one of the best stocked stashes in the building, and I was grateful for it as I retrieved a box of chocolate chip cookies and curled up under my blankets. Heaving a sigh of bliss, I grabbed my latest read, *Target Me*, off the nightstand and lost myself in a world of stalkers and kinky ex-soldier protectors.

Tomorrow would be better.

Chapter Five

Oscar

"... and she just ran off. I don't even know what I did. Can you tell me how to fix it?" I pleaded.

Elena, my second eldest sister, hummed thoughtfully.

Damn it, I knew I should have called Mom. Or maybe Tia, our eldest sister, except that Tia was at work and I was fairly sure Mom was still under the delusion I was a virgin.

Sorry, Mom, your baby boy had to grow up some time.

So that left Elena, who, while she was good for advice, loved to make me sweat more than anything.

"Tell me again about how you want to see her parts?"

"Elle, please. Just tell me what to do."

Her delighted cackle made me roll my eyes as I mentally prepared myself to cross the parking lot. I'd spotted several pigeons circling the trash can in the corner, and I was certain that fucking crow that lived in the eaves of the men's dorm was biding its time to attack me the second my defenses were down.

"Why are you breathing heavily? Are you running upstairs? Or did you just see a suspicious canary?"

"Fuck off, Elle."

Considering she was partially responsible for my aversion to birds — it wasn't a fear, I just didn't like or trust the evil shits — she could have shown a modicum of empathy. But no. I was certain that if the opportunity to lock me in an aviary ever presented itself again, she would be the first to throw away the key.

Siblings.

"Fine. If you don't want my help, I'm due to open."

"Elle!"

"Jesus, chill, little bro. Just go talk to her. Invite her to a game so she can drool all over you in all your machismo glory or whatever. She sounds like she's got problems, but I'm sure you can *fix* her, right?"

"You're the worst. You know that?"

"I know." She sighed.

I hung up, shaking my head as I took a bracing breath and power walked all the way to the rink. I didn't run; that'd be a pansy move. But it wouldn't be an overstatement to say that I was on high alert.

Just in case.

In record time, I pushed through the doors to the locker room and finally slowed my pace as a couple of the guys in various states of dress called out a greeting. I headed straight for my locker and flopped down next to Cian O'Leary, my best friend on the ice and roommate.

"Careful, O'Leary, he might want to see your parts," Foster, the prick, called to a chorus of chuckles. Brilliant. I was hoping everyone was too wasted to notice my moment of humiliation. Flipping him the bird, I bent to retie my laces in an attempt to appear casual.

Nothing to see here, find someone else to harass.

"What happened with you and the dancer last night? You two looked pretty cozy before she took off and left you with your cock in your hand."

Fuck, Foster didn't know when to give it a rest.

"And by cozy, he means you looked like you were eating her face." Cunningham chortled. Great, Dumb and Dumber were teaming up today. Before I could form a decent retort, Coach barreled into the room and started tallying his curse word quota for the day.

"What the fuck are you lazy fucks doing in here, acting like fucking ladies of leisure or some shit? Get into the fucking gym and work on those noodle dick arms of yours. This is college hockey, not a prepubescent circle jerk. Move your asses."

No one could inspire a team like Coach Markson.

Hustling to the treadmill in the center's state-of-the-art gym, my mind wandered back to Mia. I'd only just met her, but there was something about her. Did she give off damaged vibes? Ok, a little, but I certainly wasn't looking to fix her, no matter what Elle said.

She could be onto something with the invite, though. I knew I was impressive on the ice; I wouldn't be part of the team if I wasn't. I was a hard hitter and a decent striker, and I knew Cian wasn't the only player that NHL scouts would be watching this season. My manager was confident this would be the year I could go pro… if that's what I wanted.

Last year would have been the year, except…

No. I wasn't going to think about that.

The choice to stay and finish out my degree was a far better option than relying solely on a career in the majors. Almost every week, professional players in sports all around the world suffered career ending injuries that left them in second rate jobs. Tia was proof of that. I loved my eldest sister, but I couldn't imagine working in a pizza joint to make ends meet while I picked up the pieces of a career destroying knee injury. No, thank you.

From soccer balls to dough balls in an instant.

Silver eyes flashed in my mind's eye, and I nearly stumbled, grabbing onto the handrails to get my feet under me before cranking up the speed to punish myself for the distraction.

I was going to ask Mia to our next game, even if it meant hunting her down after practice.

***

First up was a punishing workout, followed by a strategy meeting that went far longer than it should have due to Foster's ability to get under Coach's skin. When the guys insisted on a team lunch at the local diner before we rested up for the game, I jumped at the chance of real food.

"I'm gonna have a mac and cheese and a philly cheese steak sandwich. Oh, and a burger with fries. I hope they have the cherry pie out today. They make the best one in the country, did you know that?" Foster bounced around the back seat of Cian's truck as we pulled up to the curb outside The Oak Diner.

"Are you planning on skating? Or sliding across the ice on your belly tonight?" Cian asked, killing the engine and sliding out.

"Nah, you got it wrong. He needs that much food to run his mouth," I joked, slamming the passenger door and rounding the truck to meet them on the sidewalk.

"You guys are hilarious. I'll eat it all and still outskate the both of you."

O'Leary and I shared a look. "Twenty bucks says you can't eat all that and keep up tonight."

Coach was going to kill us.

"Deal." Foster grinned. "Easiest twenty bucks I've ever made."

I laughed as we pushed through the door into the diner. Most of the formica tabletops were empty. Freshly wiped and ready for the next rush on whatever greasy food the Oak Hills population could possibly dream of. The air was heavy with the smell of bacon, and my mouth watered at the thought of eating almost anything after training. In the back corner, a familiar black head popped up at the sound of my laugh, and I wondered if the hockey gods were smiling on me. Or maybe freaking cupid was having a laugh, because as I looked again, it seemed the only patron in the diner we'd chosen was the exact girl I wanted to find.

Clapping O'Leary on the shoulder, I left them to pick a table and sauntered over to her.

She had a white coffee mug clasped between her hands, her head bent over it in a way that spoke of exhaustion. Had she struggled to sleep as much as I had? Though she didn't watch my approach, I saw the way her shoulders stiffened as I slid into the booth opposite her. Everything in me wanted to cage her in, trap her, and force her into a conversation, but that was a dick move. I wouldn't use my size to force her to listen, but God, I hoped she would anyway.

Torn between slouching back and pretending it was all good, and leaning forward so I could get just a bit closer to her, I settled for sitting bolt upright like an idiot.

"Hi," I said, feeling more and more like a tool as she continued to stare into her coffee mug.

Above us, Daniel Powter sang about having a bad day as the silence in the booth grew.

Shit, what was I doing? I should have planned my approach better instead of just barging into her booth and making demands.

"I'm sorry."

Her voice was soft, but still held the steel I'd heard on the first night. Silver eyes flashed up to me as she quirked her lips into the barest hint of a smile.

"That was a dick move I pulled last night. You were just being nice and I acted like a… Well, I screwed up a nice night, anyway." A long chunk of hair slid forward over her shoulder as she ducked her head for a sip of coffee, and I gripped my hands together to keep from reaching across the table to push it back for her.

"I'm not going to lie and say I know what happened last night, but I'm sure there was a reason. I just hope you'll give me another chance," I said.

That hint of a smile made another brief appearance, but this time, it seemed sad.

"You seem like a great guy, Oscar." She looked up into my face, leaning forward as though she wanted to add weight to the words. "A really great guy. You deserve someone who can give you everything. I'm going to be honest, I'm a train wreck of a human being. Go back to your puck bunnies and have fun. Find one who will… Find someone who sees you for who you really are before you settle down and have your two point five kids—"

"Come to my game tonight."

Mia frowned in confusion, and I couldn't say I blamed her. The average person wouldn't see the link between Mia laying out my life plan with someone else and me trying to insert her in my life. Because there wasn't a link. But I hoped like hell she'd accept the invitation because *she* saw me. I knew she did. And more importantly, from my perspective, I saw her.

"I don't —"

"No pressure. You can bring a friend or whatever, but we're playing one of the toughest teams in the league tonight and it'll be one hell of a game to watch. Just… think about it, please? If you want to hang out afterward, we can make it chill. Just get to know each other."

She opened her mouth. Closed it. Took a sip of her coffee and cleared her throat.

"I need to start work." As she pushed out of the booth, I caught her hand in a loose grip. Something she could easily break if she wanted to.

"Mia, please come and see me play."

What was I doing?

I loosened my fingers, ready to let her go and head back to the guys when her grip on my hand tightened.

"I'll come." With a quick squeeze, she broke our connection and hustled off through a kitchen door.

"Hey, Caveman, are you going to join us or keep harassing pretty girls?" Foster called across the diner. Shaking myself out of the shock those two little words had put me in, I made my way back to my teammates and picked up a menu. If Mia was going to be watching, I'd need to play my best game ever. And that meant carbs.

Chapter Six

MIA

I LAID out heaping plates of food for Oscar and his friends and tried not to think about the fact that I'd now served them in both my work roles.

Let me perform for you. I sighed. That was unfair, it wasn't like they'd intentionally come into my places of work *knowing* I was there. It was just that I worked in roles that catered to the male population. Food and sex. Well… the idea of sex, anyway.

A raucous laugh echoed through the diner and I looked over to see the redheaded guy who arrived with Oscar flush so red that he was almost purple. Oscar's sandy head was tilted back, his throat exposed as he laughed with an abandon I envied.

He was beautiful. The man moved with more grace than half the dancers I'd worked with, and his heart was bigger than Texas. I'd seen the way his teammates interacted with him, and how he'd treated them in turn.

He might treat you like that. I shoved the traitorous thought down. There were two possible outcomes if I got involved with Oscar. Either he would turn out like every other person I'd ever let close to me — with the exception of Luca — or I would destroy everything that was good about him. I'd already started at the party the other night.

So why had I agreed to go to his game?

A couple more tables worth of people trickled through the door, and as I seated them and took their orders, I could feel his eyes on me.

A gentle caress that felt protective rather than possessive.

I glanced over, and my breath caught at the look in his eyes. Scratch that. Possessive vibes were practically radiating off him. Was it hot in here?

Turning my back, I surreptitiously fanned my flushed face and tried to convince myself I didn't like the way he was getting to me.

I was an independent woman who didn't need a man to look at her like he knew she was his next meal. *Liar*.

The ping of the kitchen bell saved me from spiraling, but as I reached for the steaming hot plate of nachos, Loretta caught my hand, pulling me closer to the serving window.

Our sixty-year-old head chef was an absolute wizard with a spatula. She had a reputation as one of the best in the business, and I could confirm that her jalapeno poppers were something to go to war over.

There was one other thing she was infamous for.

"Child, that boy looks like he's going to eat you up. And he is one fine looking specimen. Tell me, are you going to be spending time with him?" Her pencil-drawn eyebrows bounced a couple of times before she leaned through the window to give him a slow once-over.

"Dang. I'll tell you, I could teach him a thing or two if you aren't going to take him up on what he's so blatantly offering you over there, sugar. Athletes have stamina, too. 'Specially the young ones."

"Loretta!" I said, trying to appear scandalized.

"You know I'm right."

"I know these nachos will get cold if I don't take them out." I scooped up the rapidly cooling plate and delivered it to a four-top of juniors with books spread across most of the available space. They grimaced in apology and flipped papers and highlighters around to make space in the middle for their food.

"Thank you," one of the guys said, cupping my elbow.

I could have sworn I heard a growl rumble through the diner, and when I glanced toward the hockey table, Oscar's eyes were narrowed on the contact. The guy didn't miss a beat.

Raising my brow at Mr. Possessive, I smiled graciously at the nacho table and moved back toward the kitchen to collect the next plate.

"You need a minute to go change? Dang, I went through menopause when you were in diapers and even my dusty old coochie took interest in the noise that boy just made."

"Can we... Loretta, you know he's being ridiculous, right? I barely know the guy and he thinks it's okay to... what? Growl at my patrons? What the hell?"

"Are you convincing me? Or yourself, child? You're doing a lot of denying of someone you can't keep your eyes off."

I shook my head with a sigh. Regardless of what Loretta thought, I was just going to the hockey game to watch a *friend* play. A friend I tried to get naked but a friend nonetheless.

And for the record, the state of my panties was no one's business but my own.

An hour and several trips to the table to both deliver and clear plates later, the hockey table filed up to the register to pay.

"So, how was everything today?" I asked in my most professional voice.

Around him, Oscar's friends all chorused some variation on good, while the man himself watched me with a small smirk playing around his lips.

"Was everything okay?"

"Delicious," he said, his eyes burning into me as he handed me a credit card.

"I'll see you tonight?"

I nodded, paying extra special attention to running his card and the insane sixty percent tip the team had apparently decided to pay.

"See you then."

As the group of athletes shuffled out the door, it felt like they let the air in behind them. Taking a deep breath, I asked Loretta to watch the floor for a second while I took a bathroom break. Her cackle followed me through the Staff Only door and all the way to the washrooms.

When I emerged a short time later feeling a whole lot fresher — shut up, Loretta — it was to see a most unwelcome face sitting at my counter.

Dark hair, cut high and tight, was the trademark of my ex-boyfriend. There was a time when I thought it made him look disciplined and a little like a boy scout. It hadn't taken long to learn it was the outward indicator of the unbending mindset he had about everything. I spent a long time wondering how I let myself be drawn into a relationship with a person like that, especially given my upbringing, but it took a therapist putting it in perspective to help me see it wasn't some latent masochistic tendencies.

Narcissists make up the rules in a game you don't know you're playing.

If I'd learned nothing else in my time in therapy, that would have been enough. My therapist recommended working on self and building a better sense of what relationships should be before pursuing one. I decided to go with the much more effective *push everyone away and you can't get hurt* tactic. It had been effective, too. Oscar was just taking a little longer to get the hint than others had.

Brady's head swung my way, as though sensing my discomfort. His mouth stretched into something I assumed other people would interpret as a charming smile and held a hand toward me in welcome.

"There she is. You're a hard woman to have a conversation with, Mia Maddren."

His eyes tightened, the only tell that he was incredibly displeased with me.

"I'm working, Brady. This will have to wait." Fisting my hands in my apron to disguise the shaking, I stepped behind the counter and checked the service window for any plates of food to deliver.

"I think it's waited long enough, actually. You've been avoiding me for days, Mia. You were never this poorly behaved when we were together."

"Well, we're not together anymore, Brady. So why don't you go find some other waitress to annoy and let me do my damn job."

"You—" He took a deep breath, visibly pushing down his temper.

"I came here to make amends, which is really difficult when you're intentionally making me angry. I've been patient. The least you can do is hear me out when I came all this way to see you."

I glanced around the diner, at the juniors who were still working on their nachos and studies, and at the table where the hockey players had just been. Maybe talking to Brady would give me some kind of closure. Maybe it would give me the courage to give Oscar a chance.

"I'm sorry, you're right. I have been avoiding you. Look, I honestly can't talk right now, but I'm going to the Fox U hockey game tonight. Why don't you come with me and we can talk then?" His deep brown eyes narrowed, and I had a thought that his eyes were the first things I'd noticed about him. The darkness had called to a broken part of me and I hadn't even questioned how quickly we spiraled into the toxic relationship we had. In hindsight, the puppy dog quality was similar to an angler fish. Seducing its prey with a bright shiny distraction so they didn't notice the teeth. I couldn't let myself forget the teeth.

"I'll pick you up at five-thirty."

"It's a home game. I can meet you at the rink."

"I'll pick. You. Up," he enunciated each word as though speaking to a wayward animal whose grasp on English was lacking. *Closure*, I reminded myself, grinding my molars to keep in the choice words that battered my throat, begging for release.

At my tight nod, his whole face melted into the charming mask that had fooled so many women before and, I assumed, after me.

"Excellent. We'll talk on our way over to the rink. See you then." He winked at me and sauntered out the door as I suppressed a shudder.

"What a piece of work that one is. I much prefer your hockey beau," Loretta called from the service window.

"I'm fairly certain Brady and Oscar are from entirely different planets. Though, they are both men, so who knows?"

Loretta clucked her tongue and passed me a bowl of jalapeno poppers I knew no one had ordered. "Preach, child."

***

Dressing for a hockey game became a difficult task when you wanted to impress the man who invited you, while simultaneously dissuading any such notions for the different man you invited to come with you. If I'd owned a Fox U jersey, it would have been an easy decision. Or perhaps not, wasn't there some *thing* about wearing a player's jersey?

Violet wasn't around to ask, and a glance at the clock told me I'd be late if I went down that rabbit hole on the internet.

Settling for jeans and a light sweater, I yanked on a cute pair of boots and took a bracing breath before heading out the door. Closure. I could have this discussion with Brady, then enjoy the game and see Oscar afterward. The butterflies in my stomach at the thought were less terrifying than they'd been before the house party.

Leaning against the red brick facade of the dormitory building, hands in pockets and a booted foot kicked up behind him, Brady looked like the bad boy out of every nineties movie. He even had the leather jacket to complete the look. He really was a handsome guy to look at.

Shame about the personality.

As I pushed through the front door, he straightened and waited for me to join him for the walk across campus.

"Mia."

"Brady."

We fell into step, and as the silence began to stretch, I cast furtive glances at him from the corner of my eye. What was this about? Luca had told him in no uncertain terms to leave me alone.

A fat crow cawed at me from its perch on a trash can, and I shuddered, praying its throaty call wasn't an omen of bad things to come.

"I want you to know something," Brady said without breaking stride or looking over.

"What's that?"

"I've changed. I went to an anger management class and started seeing a therapist."

I glanced at him in surprise. Therapy had always been a bone of contention between us because both of us needed it, but only I went.

"That's good, Brady. I'm glad you're getting some help."

I wasn't sure why he'd felt the need to drive eight hours to tell me this, though. It could have been a phone conversation, or even better, he could have just got on with his life without me entirely.

"I'm glad you think that, because we're getting back together. I've rented a house in town for us while you finish your degree, then we can go home."

My stomach dropped, the old feelings of helplessness rising like a tide I thought I'd beaten back. I couldn't do it again.

If I moved into that house, there would be no degree, no friends, no Mia. I'd return to the shell of the person I was before. Deep green eyes flashed in my mind, and I sought out the ice rink between the buildings.

I wasn't the same old Mia, and new Mia didn't have to listen to Brady's orders.

"We're not getting back together, Brady. We were good for a while, but that's gone now." The lie rose like bile in my mouth, but it was worth it to keep the peace. Just a little longer and I'd be rid of him for good.

"You're not understanding me, Mia. I changed for you. I came all the way out here and set up our house for you. Now you're telling me no? That's just... I'm really disappointed. I expected more from you, Mia."

My eyes welled with unexpected tears, and even though I *knew* it was a manipulation, the lost little girl I had been raised her head.

"I'm sorry, Brady. Look, let's start with friendship. We'll go to the game and see what happens from there. Okay?"

Brady grunted, scowling hard for a moment before his face dissolved into a smile. He reached out and wiped the tears caught in my lashes before turning us back toward the hockey rink where a crowd was milling around the doors waiting for entrance to the game.

"You can play your game of hard to get, Mia. For now."

His hand on my back felt like a warning.

We moved through the crowd to find our seats, the noise and excitement washing over us, but unable to connect. Fox U was on a winning streak, and it seemed like every man and his dog wanted a piece of the action. The huge cameras mounted around the stadium reminded me that it wasn't just those attending who would be watching. Oscar was practically a celebrity around here. So why was he getting all growly around me?

As the players took to the ice to warm up, the noise in the stadium took on even greater levels. Glancing around, I noticed they were doing a kiss-cam. Cute.

While people laughed and cheered, I was focused on a big body that looked like he was humping the ice. Several of his teammates were performing the same warmup move, but he made it feel illicit. Sandy blond hair flopped in his eyes as he looked up through the crowd and seemed to skewer me. Maintaining eye contact, he circled his knees a few more times, and I flushed as I imagined being beneath him when he did it. His lithe body was a thing of beauty, even wrapped up in all his hockey gear. It occurred to me that I may finally see the appeal of hockey. A cheer went up around me, and I was ripped from the moment by a pair of demanding lips crashing down on mine. Brady. His tongue thrust viciously between my teeth, spurred on by the cheers around us. Working my hands up between our bodies, I tried to shove him off, but his grip only tightened, taking full advantage of the moment before he released me in his own time, stepping back and giving me a contrived boyish grin.

"Had to make it good for the cameras."

I hated him.

Chapter Seven

Oscar

I PRIDED myself on being a chill guy. When you grew up as the only male in a house full of women, you got good at controlling your reaction to things, but right now, all I could see was red. Cian skated past and nudged me where I knelt, frozen on the ice as some douchebag mouth-raped Mia. I had to get to her. That fucking kiss-cam was nothing more than a convenient excuse for dickhead guys to take advantage of the girls around them.

"Caveman! Get your head out of your ass. It's game time." O'Leary pulled up in front of me, the ice whining under his skates. Game time. Right.

But the aggression wouldn't leave me. I felt as though I couldn't breathe until I'd checked in with Mia. What if she was upset? If she was hurt? Sometimes it was the smallest thing that could push the sadness I saw behind her eyes to overflow, and I couldn't handle losing someone else to it.

"Oscar." Cian was in my face as though he'd been there for a while.

"Come on, man."

I sought Mia's face out in the crowd, but she wasn't where I'd seen her last.

Cian let out a huff and skated off to take his position for the face-off. The only thing that kept me on the ice was the fact that douchebag was exactly where he had been, smirking down at me like he knew something I didn't. Well, fuck him very much.

With a deep breath to try to find my center, I took my position and waited for the game to start.

O'Leary won the puck drop and broke past the left D-man, headed for the goal crease with Danthorpe U's players hot on his tail. Danthorpe's right defenseman closed in to intercept, and I put on a burst of speed, carrying the big guy hard into the boards as O'Leary sailed past and scored off a wraparound that Danthorpe's goalie didn't see coming.

"Good goal," I called as he skated by.

"Yeah, well, any time you want to make yourself available for a pass would be great. Switch on, man. Don't leave me out here alone."

"Yeah, switch on, man," Danthorpe's right defenseman chirped in my ear.

"Fuck off."

"You should have been penalized on that body check. Must be fucking nice to have the referee in your pocket."

I ignored him, chasing the puck, which was sailing across the center line after a rebound shot off the boards from Andrews. He was right, but hell if I'd admit it. I should have been sitting in the penalty box, not passing the biscuit to O'Leary for an assist. The same fucking D-man intercepted my pass and flung the biscuit to his center before I could check his ass.

The game continued in much the same way. The right defenseman getting in my ear every time we took the ice, and me letting my temper reign until late in the second period when I spotted Mia in the crowd.

"That's the kiss-cam chick, right? Fuck, she looks like she'd be fun to ride. I can show her a real good time."

Between one blink and the next, my gloves and stick were on the ice, my hands wrapped in his jersey as I hauled back, ready to shut him up with my fist.

"Easy there, Caveman," O'Leary murmured, wrapping one arm around me, while trapping my fist with his other.

"I will make your life hell if you get ejected from this game. Relax. Right now."

Relaxing in his grip, I waited for Cian to let me go before collecting my gloves and stick, and heading to the penalty box to serve out my five minutes for roughing.

Danthorpe's D-man smirked, sending me a mocking wave before skating off to set up for a power play.

Flopping onto the bench, I let my head fall back against the wall, then repeated the motion a few more times in hopes of shifting my funk. I couldn't do this to my team. I had to get my head in the game. On the other side of the rink, in the third row back from the boards, I spotted Mia standing alone in a sea of faces screaming and hissing at the players on the ice. Her face was pale, and despite the frozen arena, I got the inkling she wasn't cold. Her face was blank, as though a mask had dropped over her features, concealing anything that was Mia from the outside world, but her eyes were what stopped me dead. The look in them finally cut through my reckless anger and forced me to tighten my control for the rest of the game.

Because if I ever saw that look again, it would be too soon.

***

Coach tore shreds off me the second we got off the ice. We'd won the game — no thanks to me — but my behavior was "the kind of shit that kept kids from going pro."

Worse was when I made it to the locker room and saw my teammates looking at me like I was a stranger. I'd lost my damn mind over this girl. The problem was... I still couldn't let it go. There was some part of me that needed to know she was okay, because that look on her face had been really close to fear.

Showering quickly, I threw my things together and headed out of the change rooms. I'd already had my debrief: I played like an idiot. Cian caught my shoulder before I could slip out the locker room doors. "You have to find your chill, man. Whatever is going on with you is worrying the team."

I brushed his hand off.

"I know what I'm doing. I just had an off night. It's all good, I promise," I lied. He narrowed his eyes like he could see through my bullshit, but stepped back.

"Just remember you're not alone. I don't want you to go back to where you were last year."

"I'm not. I won't." Shit, I hadn't thought about that. They were all worried I'd backslide.

"It's nothing like that, I promise." It was my turn to squeeze his shoulder, and as I did, I felt some of the tension leave my roommate.

"I'll see you a bit later. Enjoy the afterparty."

"You can't save everyone, Oscar. It's not your place to try, either."

Slapping him on the back in farewell, I slipped out the doors and searched the crowd for the one face I needed to see more than my next breath. Cian was right, I couldn't save everyone. That was a physical impossibility, but I would damn well try my hardest to save Mia.

Stepping out into the mass of humanity outside the locker room, I searched every face for the one I needed to see.

"Oscar!" My name was chorused by several people, both male and female, as I pushed through the masses and came out the other side empty-handed. She was nowhere to be found, and it occurred to me that I didn't even have her number.

Cursing my own stupidity, I paced outside the rink before deciding I needed backup.

Cameron Jones was the smartest person I knew. He was the point guard for Fox U's basketball team and my best friend since childhood. Where Cian knew me better than anyone on the ice, Cam knew me better than me, and his insight was something I could appreciate around about now. Even if he just told me I was an idiot, like Coach did.

Despite the fact it was nine PM on a Saturday, I didn't hesitate to hammer on his dorm door. Predictably, he answered moments later wearing basketball shorts and a sweater and looking a little ruffled.

"Hey man, I need your help." I pushed past him, the story spilling out of me as I flopped onto his bed.

"— and she's gone. I don't have her number, or any idea where she's staying. I'm going to lose my mind if I have to wait until Monday to see her in class, so what's my choice here? Hang out in front of the girls' dorm for the next two days like a creeper and pray she doesn't live off campus? Ask every girl I see if they can steer me in the right direction? And if I see her, what do I say? I'm sorry I turned into a crazy person, because the sight of someone else's hands on you made me murderous? Cam, please help me."

"I don't —" Cam started, but he was interrupted by a second voice.

"You need to go talk to her, first of all."

I frowned, lifting my head and noticing a small blonde perched on the spare bed.

"I, uh. Hi. Sorry, man. I didn't realize you had company." I divided a sheepish grin between the two and sat up, letting my hands hang between my knees.

"It's all good, Violet, this lovesick idiot is Oscar. Oscar, Violet is getting help with math."

She cringed at the word, and a small thread of amusement snaked through me.

"Not a numbers girl, huh? I get it. Life's too short for quadratic equations, right?" Cam snorted while Violet looked like someone was finally making sense.

"So you like this girl," Cam said, getting us back on track.

"There's something about her. I want to get to know her, you know? But it feels like every time I take a step forward, she takes three back. Christ, that kind of makes me sound like a stalker, yeah? But there's something there, and it feels like she's giving me just enough to want to chase. Hell, maybe I'm the one being played." I dropped my head into my hands. I couldn't get my head straight, so I couldn't imagine how they could understand.

"Oscar." Violet's voice was tentative, and she waited until I'd made eye contact to continue.

"Are you in it for the chase? Or do you genuinely want to see what could be between you?"

"Definitely the second one. I don't… Look, Violet, I'll be honest. I don't need to chase women, I'm a hockey player, but Mia…" I threw up my hands and wondered if I'd ever get my head straight. She eyed me for a long moment before nodding.

"Okay, so here's what you're going to do. Go into town and get Thai food. Anything spicy with noodles will be her jam. She's in room four oh three. Don't forget the prawn crackers."

I gaped at her. Could it really be that easy? Cam shrugged.

"Taking her food seems like a solid plan, at least it should get you through the door. After that, you'll have to rely on your personality."

I punched him in the arm as a grin slid over my face. I had a plan, and I knew where to find her. This could work.

Chapter Eight

Mia

THE IMAGE of Oscar sitting in that box, his face a thundercloud as blood dripped from his nose was lodged in my head long after I left the ice rink. I was no stranger to violence, but the rage that had radiated off Oscar since the stupid kiss-cam incident was scary. The second I'd managed to break the kiss, I'd stormed outside and insisted Brady leave. He'd had his say and I was done playing nice with him. After threats, platitudes and a whole host of dramatics, Brady had finally found somewhere else to be, and I'd walked back inside in time to see Oscar throw his gloves onto the ice and start swinging at a guy in a blue jersey wearing number twenty-three on his back.

I popped a Swedish Fish in my mouth and grimaced. I needed to eat some real food, but the idea of going out and ordering something held no appeal.

A knock at the door interrupted my snack-based musings, and I frowned, unsure who would be coming around at this time of night. Violet was studying with her new tutor and had implied it would be a late one. No one else knew my room number, unless Brady had bribed someone.

Praying I wasn't about to walk into another run-in with my ex, I pulled a sweater over my pajamas and opened the door.

A waft of chili and soy sauce made my nose tingle and my mouth water as I glimpsed a white bag of takeout grasped in my visitor's hand. Large knuckles peeked out from beneath Fox U's signature orange, white, and black sweatshirt. Dragging my attention away from the delicious offering — and if I were being honest, I didn't just mean the food — I looked up into bright green eyes that looked distinctly sheepish.

"Hi," Oscar said, holding the plastic bag out toward me. "I come bearing food."

"Who told you?" I asked, eyeing the bag and wondering if I could steal the food and slam the door before he had time to react. Nah, I wasn't that fast, or skilled, and I knew for a fact after seeing him on the ice that his reflexes were killer. If I wanted the food, I'd have to play nice. And I really wanted the food. There was only one thing missing.

"If I can come in and talk, I'll give you these." From behind his back, he pulled a bag full of pink shells of happiness.

Someone had definitely ratted me out, but the longer I stood in the doorway, the smell of Thai in my nose and the promise of prawn crackers dangled in front of me, the less I cared.

I stepped back, snatching the bag from his fingers as he passed the threshold and shoved a cracker in my mouth, enjoying the way it melted on my tongue. A lot of people didn't appreciate the simplicity of the crackers, but growing up, this was as close to gourmet as Luca and I got.

Closing the door, I turned to find Oscar watching me closely.

"So… what brings you here? Not that I'm not grateful for the food delivery, but I thought you'd be celebrating your win," I said, skirting around him and stalling out when I realized we had one desk chair or the beds to sit on. I settled for sinking to the mat cross-legged, leaning my back against my mattress. Oscar followed my lead and stretched his legs out before unpacking a feast worth of food between us.

"Did you order every noodle dish on the menu?" I asked, inspecting each of the boxes in wonder. Oscar rubbed a palm over the back of his neck, the sheepish look back on his face in full force.

"Maybe? The way you disappeared, I felt like I might owe you an apology."

"Why would you need to apologize to me? We don't know each other," I said, avoiding his eyes.

"Maybe not yet, but we will."

Taking a deep breath, I chose a spicy rice noodle dish and pasted on a smile.

"Well, you didn't need to worry, I'm just fine."

"Mia, I grew up in a house full of women. I know what fine means. But you're right, we don't know each other, so let's start simple. What's your major?"

He picked his own dish, snapped apart his set of chopsticks and shoveled a ridiculous amount of egg noodles into his mouth like he'd been eating with sticks for years. Hell, maybe he had. I played with my wooden fork, prising apart my rice noodles while I debated the risks of 'getting to know' Oscar Cavanaugh.

Dangerous was the conclusion I kept coming to, but it didn't keep me from answering him.

"Psychology."

"Oh, cool. So are you trying to fix yourself or save the world?" Oscar asked, flashing me a grin that seemed to melt off his face as he caught my reaction.

"Sorry, you don't have to answer that. It's just what my mom always said. People get into mental health to understand their own shit or to fix everyone else's. It's dumb. Sorry. Gee, this food is good, isn't it?" He cut off his babbling by shoving another load of noodles into his mouth, puffing his cheeks like an adorable squirrel.

I was learning that Oscar Cavanaugh had no filter, and I kind of liked it.

"I guess a little of both? How about you?" I asked, crunching on another prawn cracker.

"Exercise science. If the NHL don't come knocking this year, I want to become a strength and conditioning coach. Even if I do start out playing, I only have so many good years in me, but helping others achieve their best would be an awesome way to make a living."

I nodded, liking how his eyes lit up when he spoke about his degree.

"So you're a bit of a nerd, then? Isn't that an oxymoron? A nerdy jock?"

Oscar grinned. "Hardly a nerd, but I might be able to teach you a thing or two. How are you finding sports psych, anyway?"

"Hard, but good. I guess I understand a lot of what she's telling us because I've heard it from my brother."

Oscar perked up, clearly ready to take advantage of the conversational pathway I accidentally dropped.

"You mentioned your brother the other day. Is he in sports?"

"Yeah, swimming, actually. He's on the national team."

Oscar shuffled down until he was spread out on his side, one elbow beneath him as he scooped up more noodles. His box was almost empty, but I guessed a hockey game took a lot out of you. Especially the way he was playing. The reminder of how violently he had played washed over me like a bucket of cold water. There was a reason I'd left the game early, and it had nothing to do with Brady acting like an ass before he took off.

"Where did you go?" Oscar asked carefully, setting aside his food and ducking his head to see my face.

"Nowhere. I just… it's late, isn't it? Don't you have to get up early for practice tomorrow?"

Oscar frowned. "We have a late start. Seriously, if you want me to leave, I will, but if it's something we can talk about…"

"You were really rough today. Is hockey always that… violent?" The words left me without permission, and as they hit home with him, I wished I could call them back. I knew it was my fault he'd been in that mood, that if I

61

hadn't told Brady to come with me, he wouldn't have ended up in the penalty box.

"Yeah, I had a bad night. I was stuck in my head, but that's my own fault. I'm sorry if I scared you."

I opened my mouth. Closed it. Thought back on his explanation. He hadn't accused me of throwing off his game. Hadn't insisted it was my fault. In fact, he'd taken responsibility and apologized for it.

Rocking onto my knees, I leaned across the space between us and pressed my lips to his in the most genuine kiss I'd ever given anyone. Before he could react, I pulled back, pressing my fingertips to my mouth in an effort to keep his warmth with me.

Surprise morphed into a pleased grin on his face as he sat up and faced me.

"What was that for?"

I shrugged. How could I tell him what a rarity he was in my world? That just being around him made me feel hopeful?

I settled for telling him, "Just for being you. Don't change."

He nodded, accepting the explanation and swiveled his body so we were facing each other across the space between the beds.

"Okay, so your brother is an Olympic swimmer. What about other family? Siblings? Parents? Step parents?"

I barely suppressed a shudder, turning his question back on him before he realized what a sore spot he'd hit on.

"You grew up in a house full of girls. How was that?"

Oscar barked a laugh, shifting into another position on the floor. Was he uncomfortable? Or just incapable of keeping still?

"Messy. My dad died before I was born, so I came into the family as the man of the house, but because there was a three-year age gap between Elena and me, I was also the girl's favorite doll. I always had more clothes than any guy could know what to do with, and I've been on bathroom cleanup since I learned to shave. Apparently, the whiskers I left on the sink trumped three women shedding hair twenty-four seven around the house. I swear Tia sheds more than Mom's labrador."

I laughed at the image he painted. Though his words sounded like a complaint, his eyes shone with affection and the smile hadn't left his face.

"My mom is the strongest person I know. She raised all three of us while working a full-time job and we didn't want for anything. We've always been really close. I mean, we fought, sure. I still argue with Elle, but that's because she's part demon and lives to torment me... aaand I'm talking too much."

I chuckled, stretching my legs out alongside his.

"No, I like it. Okay, what's your greatest fear?"

"Birds." No hesitation. He threw it out so quickly I wasn't sure whether it was the truth or an ongoing joke.

"Birds?"

He nodded.

"Those evil fuckers are everywhere. Flying around and just waiting for a time to strike. If I ever disappear, it'll be because that crow outside our dorm got me. He's been biding his time, waiting for the opportunity to clean my bones and wear my skin. You can see it in its beady eyes."

The earnest look on his face startled a laugh out of me.

"Okay, birds are the devil's minions. Got it. Anything else?"

"Oh no, it's your turn, Miss Maddren. I told you my fear, now what's yours?"

I pulled my knees in toward my chest, the smile sliding off my face as I contemplated lying. Oscar had been so open, it was only fair that I give him a little of the same.

"People."

He shifted around until we were side by side again, curiosity clearly making him antsy but, to his credit, he didn't dig.

"I get it, people suck. What's your favorite weekend activity?"

And that was it. We talked about our likes and dislikes, our hobbies, and more about Oscar's family until the Thai food was ice cold and the lock on my door clicked open. Violet froze in the threshold, clearly surprised to find me awake, but the look she shot Oscar made me think his presence was less unexpected.

"Hey, it's you," Oscar said, climbing to his feet.

Violet closed the door behind her and held her hands up.

"Guilty."

"So it was you who ratted me out," I said, climbing up far less gracefully than Oscar. Without a word, he reached down and helped me get my feet under me.

"You've been hiding too much lately, it was time someone gave you a kick in the ass," she said unapologetically, coming over to inspect the remains of our meal.

As Violet helped herself to our leftovers, Oscar stood in the middle of our space looking a little lost.

"I guess I should get going," he said slowly, watching my face in that way I was starting to enjoy.

"I guess so."

I walked him to the door, holding it for him as he ambled out into the hall.

Somewhere further down the hall, someone wolf-whistled. "Looking good, Caveman. If you're finished in there, do you wanna come have some fun with us?"

I gritted my teeth, reminding myself I didn't do jealousy. Oscar made it a lot easier by completely ignoring the commentary. He grasped the doorframe over my head, folding his six foot four frame in half until we were eye to eye.

"Spend the day with me tomorrow. Please."

"I have to work in the morning." The refusal, while true, came out like a shot aimed to hurt.

Catching myself in the defensive act, I softened the rejection.

"But I have the afternoon free, if your training doesn't last all day."

He grinned as though he'd passed some sort of test and pecked a kiss on my cheek, backing up before I could react.

"I'll see you tomorrow, then. Wait. Can I give you my number?"

Now that I knew he'd been raised by women, it seemed obvious. Apart from his possessive tendencies, he was incredibly respectful and in tune with his emotions in a way that I hadn't seen in many other men. Luca was a closed book about everything. Hell, I was the only person allowed to touch him without losing a limb.

Retrieving my cell from my back pocket, I unlocked the screen and handed it over.

He plugged in the digits and handed it back with a smirk.

"You didn't call yourself?"

"If you want me to have your number, you can give it to me. If you don't, then that's your prerogative."

"Does this work on all the girls?" I asked, needing to remind myself he was no blushing freshman and this could all be a ruse to suck me in.

In response, Oscar fished his cell out of his own pocket, opened the contacts and handed it to me.

I scrolled through the names of his team, his sisters and mom, and a couple of other men's contacts. There was only one other female name in there. Katie.

"I don't give my number to a lot of people. If they want me, they can find me on the ice."

Handing back his phone, I smiled and took a step back toward my room.

"Have a good night, Mia," he said, accepting the end of our conversation and I waited until he'd walked the length of the corridor before I closed the door.

Violet watched me curiously as I stood frozen, staring at my phone. Instinct was telling me I could trust him, but trauma screamed it wasn't worth it.

Do the hard thing.

It was another of my therapist's words of wisdom, and I knew that she was right. I couldn't grow in comfort. I had to take the chance. Clicking call on his number, my heart pounded as I waited to hear his voice.

"Hello?"

"I wanted to give you my number."

There was a short pause, then the sound of his footsteps chuffing along on the ground. When he spoke, I could hear the smile in his voice.

"I'm really glad to hear that. I'll see you tomorrow, okay?"

"As long as the crow doesn't get you."

"Don't even joke about that, I'm right near his lair. Good night, Mia."

"Good night, Oscar."

Chapter Nine

O<small>SCAR</small>

T<small>HE</small> <small>HIGH</small> <small>OF</small> spending time with Mia and getting her number carried me through training the next day. Coach was still pissed about my performance on the ice the night before and took it out on all of us with a grueling session. Cian was quieter than usual; his characteristic banter absent in the locker room. Shit. I owed the guys big time. These were my brothers and I'd fucked up.

I cleared my throat, waiting for the guys to look over before I opened my mouth and realized I had no idea how to make it right.

"I fucked up last night," I started.

"Are you planning on making a habit of it?" Fraser asked. I took in the faces around me. Guys I'd worked with for years to build the team we had today. They deserved my best, and last night, I hadn't delivered. Would I do it again? Definitely not, if I could help it.

"Well…no…"

"Then we're all good. If you need anything, just let us know."

"Just don't take it onto the ice next time," Cian piped up, throwing his sweat-soaked undershirt at my head. I dodged the missile, grimacing at the wet splat it made against the locker behind me.

"Thanks, guys."

"Are we going to hug now?" Fraser asked, holding his arms wide.

"Hell yes, we are." I tackled him before he could renege. I had no problem telling my people I loved them, and man hugs were good for the soul. Fraser sighed in mock resignation as I lifted him off his feet for good measure, making the other guys chuckle.

When I turned toward Cian, he gave me a sly smile before offering his fist for a bump. Whatever, I'd take the forgiveness for now and write up an IOU on his hug for later.

After a long hot shower and debrief with Coach about what to expect for the coming week, Cian and I were crossing the parking lot when my phone chimed.

Balloon Girl: Finishing at 3 meet you at the diner?

I'll be there *wink emoji*

Balloon Girl: Wear something pretty, I'm taking you out.

Ooh, I'll make sure I'm presentable, then.

"WHO ARE YOU TEXTING? Wait. Never mind. It's the dancer, isn't it?" Cian said, eyeing the goofy look I could feel on my face.

"Her name's Mia, and don't be jealous. There's always a place for you in my life."

"First Cam, and now her. At this rate, I'm going to be the last person who finds out you're in the hospital."

I looked over at him in shock.

"Why the hell would I be in the hospital?"

Cian furrowed his brow and shrugged, as though even he didn't understand where his thoughts had gone.

"Just like, you know, the important people are the ones that hear first if something's wrong. Forget it. I'm being dumb."

I threw my arm around his shoulders, ignoring his attempt to dodge me.

"You're not being dumb. You're still one of my best friends, man. If I ever end up in the hospital, you'll know. But if you're hanging around waiting for this bubble butt, just know I may be an organ donor, but I still want you to buy me dinner first." I slapped his flat ass as he shoved me off him.

"You're the worst when you're in a good mood. Go see your girl and leave me alone."

I cackled, breaking off from him and heading toward my truck parked in the center of the parking lot, well away from the crow and his murder trash can.

***

Mia was behind the counter when I arrived at the diner ten minutes later. She was facing the window to the kitchen, laughing at something when the bell above my head gave away my presence. Her long, dark hair was pulled back in a long ponytail, the strands flowing over her shoulders as her head moved. Even in all black and an apron, she looked like she had just stepped out of a magazine, and I wondered what the hell I'd done right to get her to notice me.

As I approached the counter, Mia glanced back at the kitchen window and scowled, her hand waving as though she were shushing someone before she turned toward me with one brow arched.

"This is you dressing pretty? Really?" she asked, her eyes sliding down the length of my body. My lips spread in a wicked grin as her perusal slowed down the lower it got.

"I have it on good authority that women appreciate men in sweatpants."

Mia hummed; her focus caught on the pants in question. If she kept it up, I'd have to slide into one of those booths. As comfortable as the pants were, they telegraphed boners like nobody's business.

"My eyes are up here, Balloon Girl," I said when Mr. Happy started to take notice of the attention he was receiving.

Mia flushed a pretty shade of pink, and I heard the distinct sound of a chuckle coming through the kitchen service window.

"Ah, can I get you something to eat while you wait? I still have an hour to go."

"Sure."

I ended up eating more than I should have. Loaded fries and a burger led into pie and a shake, and by the time Mia had cleared everything away, I felt like convincing her to take an afternoon nap with me. But she had decided to plan our first date, and I wasn't going to spoil it by being a lump.

"You ready?" she asked, bouncing out of the Staff Only section, wearing a red and black summer dress underneath a heavy black coat.

"Are you going to be warm enough?" I asked, mentally slapping myself because who was I to stop her exposing a set of legs like that? Long and muscled, I could imagine them wrapping around my... sweatpants! I was seriously regretting my choice of clothing as I covered my groin to avoid everyone seeing the effect my imagination was having on me.

We climbed into my truck and Mia directed me out onto the highway, explaining the place she had in mind was a couple of towns over. While we drove, she plugged her phone into my stereo and blasted showtunes, all of which she sang along to. Her voice was smooth and a little husky when she hit the high notes, and I wondered if she sang in her burlesque performances. When I asked, she got quiet and pointed out a turnoff instead of answering.

One day, she would trust me with her secrets, and I was sure it would be worth the wait. In the meantime, I was going to enjoy watching her open up.

She directed me to pull in at a strip mall that looked like it had seen better days, the paint peeling on several signs. A tattoo shop on the corner was the only business that appeared to be open. Undiscouraged by the filth and all the "keep out" vibes the place was rocking, Mia was positively glowing as she pulled me down an alleyway between a cosmetic surgery shopfront and a drugstore and out into a small courtyard.

"Through here," she said, grinning at me as she opened a wrought iron gate.

"Are we allowed to be here?" I asked, looking around and wishing I had a stick or something with me, just in case. I wasn't a fighter, but I could swing a stick like nobody's business. Mia's laugh rang off the walls and warmed me, despite my nerves screaming we weren't safe.

"Of course we are. Come on, she's expecting us."

Without hesitation, Mia pushed through a door inset with stained glass windows and marched down a narrow hallway, her heels clicking on the polished floorboards. The hall opened into a large room lined with mirrors, a sound system in one corner and a tall, stately looking woman in a black dress directly in front of us. Mia closed the distance between them and hugged the woman before turning and beckoning me closer.

"Oscar, this is Francesca. She's been teaching me dance for a few years now and offered to give us a lesson together. If you're up for it, that is."

The glint of challenge in her eye was subtle, but enough to make me want to laugh. She thought she had me, but this was about to get interesting.

"What are we learning?"

"Bachata," Francesca announced, giving Mia a no-nonsense look at her squeak of protest.

"I was thinking a waltz or something," she said, looking between me and her friend. I wondered what exactly we were getting into, but it couldn't be that bad.

Two years of tap with Elle was bad. And something I would take to my grave, because no one should have that kind of leverage over another human being.

Francesca clicked at me, pointing to Mia as she worked a clicker that made the lights dim. Music floated in through invisible speakers.

"You. Hold her close, knee between her legs. No, closer." Grunting, she positioned us how she wanted, and I sucked in a quick breath, cursing my sweatpants again as my thigh pressed up against Mia's core.

"Now, swivel hips left right left, then right left right." Francesca demonstrated once before coming up behind us and manually moving our hips. I got the hang of the choreography quickly, but being so close to Mia, staring down into those silver eyes, meant that I kept losing track of the beat. Francesca was relentless, correcting posture, and even slapping my ass at one point when my semi-hard cock brushed against Mia's hip, and I stumbled, trying to conceal the effect she was having on me.

"You got a little problem there, Caveman?" Mia murmured as Francesca left the room, muttering about lost causes.

"There's nothing little about it," I said with a smirk. Unbidden, my hands ran down the curve of her hips and back up to the dip of her waist. God, Jessica Rabbit had nothing on this girl's curves and having spent the previous hour holding them like I owned them, I wanted nothing more than to take her back to my truck and show her exactly how big my 'problem' was.

"I could help you with it, if you wanted." She cupped my erection through my sweats, pulling a groan from my throat, even as my eyes flew to the hall Francesca had disappeared down.

"You have no idea how much I want your hands on me, but we're not alone," I said, stepping back with a herculean amount of willpower. My dick screamed at me that I was an idiot who didn't deserve the minx in front of me, and I knew he was right, but it also wasn't the time.

Last time we'd gotten close, I'd fucked things up, and I wasn't going to let that happen again.

Mia nodded, her eyes dropping to my groin as her tiny, pink tongue shot out to wet her bottom lip. A new level of arousal shot through me, my dick twitching at the attention, and I cupped both hands over him to stop any more bright ideas.

"Mia, seriously. You need to stop looking at me like that before I put you on your knees and say to hell with Francesca. I'm trying to be a gentleman here."

The noise that came out of her throat was nothing short of a purr, and I knew I was done for.

Grasping her hand, I pulled her out of the house and back down the alley to where my truck waited, thankfully untouched. We climbed into the back seat, both of us racing for some silently agreed upon endpoint. The second the door slammed behind us, I pulled her toward me and crashed my mouth down on hers. This was closer to the first night we'd been together, except that Mia felt like she was here with me this time. Everything felt richer, stronger. Her soft lips were pliant beneath mine, her tongue thrusting into my mouth and giving as good as she got.

"Fuck, you're beautiful. Can I see you?"

She shushed me, placing a finger over my lips as she cupped my cock with her other hand, stroking hard enough to make me arch beneath her.

"I want to taste you. Can I, Oscar?" she asked, her silver eyes partially covered by a curtain of her hair.

"I'm yours. Do whatever you want to me," I said, lifting my hips to help her move my sweats out of the way. With no hesitation, her lips slipped over my head and all the way down until her nose brushed my lower stomach and I strained to keep still. The warmth of her mouth was heaven. Moving slowly, she raised her head, the flat of her tongue pressing hard on the underside of my dick until she reached the head and flicked at the slit like she was enjoying an ice cream.

"Mia," I said, my voice nothing but gravel as she hummed and worked her mouth over me again.

Fuck, I wasn't going to last. It was too good. She was too good. I brushed her hair away from her face, watching greedily as her pink lips stretched around my girth.

"You're too good for me. Fuck." I thrust shallowly, unable to keep still and stroked her head.

"Babe, I'm going to come unless you stop."

Mia hummed and, on her next upward stroke, used her teeth to scrape my sensitive flesh.

Game. Over.

"Mia—"

My last attempt at a chivalrous warning cut off with a long groan as my stomach tensed and I shot my load down that pretty throat of hers.

While I caught my breath, Mia sat up, swiveling to lean against the door and watch while I recovered.

"I'm sorry," I said as soon as I could breathe again.

"That was kind of the point, you know," she said, a smile tugging at the corner of her mouth.

I nodded, still feeling stupid after the intensity of the orgasm she had given me.

"Give me a minute and I'll return the favor."

"Oh, you don't need to do that," she said, folding into herself. I looked past her, to the parking lot outside my truck and wanted to curse myself.

"I'm sorry, I wasn't thinking. Did you have anything else planned? Or can I take you to dinner?"

Mia sighed and unfurled herself, crawling across the seat to straddle my lap. She wrapped her arms around me and tucked her head beneath my chin in a hug that I happily returned.

"You are something else, Oscar Cavanaugh. I don't deserve you, but I'm scared I won't have a choice but to keep you."

"I hope you do," I murmured, stroking a hand down her hair and enjoying the moment of closeness.

Chapter Ten

MIA

THIS WAS the first night in a week I hadn't seen Oscar, and I found his absence made me edgy. The hockey team had left early in the morning for a five-hour road trip to play against the Wolves on their home turf. I hadn't followed hockey until I started hanging out with Oscar, but just a little research had left me scared for him. This team was known for playing dirty and more than once, opposing teams had been injured in fan riots after their team lost a game. I'd made Oscar swear he'd be safe before he left and, from what I'd seen of the game, he'd been true to his word. The temper I'd seen barely contained in the last game was completely gone. The camera had even caught a closeup of him laughing with an opposing player. I glanced down at my phone where I'd snapped a photo of the closeup, his head thrown back, mouthguard visible beneath his helmet. His eyes sparkled with the kind of mirth I was coming to expect from him. Despite his nickname, Oscar was intelligent and self-aware. He made people feel like they mattered and everything was right with the world as long as he was smiling. Catching the train of my thoughts, I dropped my phone on my bed as though it could burn me.

Violet was out studying again, and the silence of the room felt almost suffocating. It was my night to dance at Madame Cognac's burlesque, but I'd called and begged off. The idea of dancing while I felt so raw was not something I wanted anyone to see.

Maybe one person, a voice whispered in the back of my head. Shoving a cookie in my mouth to quiet it, I flopped back on my bed and retrieved my cell, my attention drawn back to Oscar's smiling face.

Vibrations shook my hand a moment later and a glance at the top of my screen showed Oscar was requesting a video call. Despite wearing nothing but an old shirt, I accepted the call and laid back as his smiling face filled the screen.

"Hey there, Balloon Girl. I wasn't sure if I'd get you or not."

"Yeah, I took the night off. Had some unmissable TV to watch."

He straightened against what looked like a wooden bedhead. "You watched the game?"

I nodded, rolling to my stomach to give my arm a rest.

"I did, but considering how close you came to getting your throat cut by that skate, I almost wish I didn't."

He chuckled, running a hand over his stubbled jaw and down his intact throat. It had been a terrifying moment. He'd passed the puck off as he slid headfirst into the boards, while a Wolves player had barely stopped his skates in time. Oscar's face had been covered in ice shavings when he found his feet, but he'd just taken a moment to remove his helmet and wipe his face, then got back to it like he hadn't almost died on national TV.

"It was fine. I'm sure it looked a lot worse than it was," Oscar said, settling back and hooking a hand behind his head.

"I believe you're missing a shirt, Mr. Cavanaugh," I said, noticing the stretch of bare skin exposed with the shift of his phone.

"I just got out of the shower. Don't worry, I'm still wearing those sweats you liked so much last week." He shifted his camera down, the picture taking a slow stroll over miles of tight muscle until I got a good view of the gray sweats he'd worn to dance in and the impressive bulge beneath them. I swallowed hard, my mouth watering at the memory of the taste of him.

I'd never been a huge fan of blow jobs with Brady, but there had been something about making Oscar come undone. The way he tried so hard to be respectful. I'd felt powerful for the first time in a very, very long time, and I wanted more of it.

"Are you alone right now?" I asked, trying to make the question sound innocent when my intentions were anything but.

"Ahh, yeah. I'm sharing the room with Cian, but he went out to celebrate. I doubt he'll be back for a while."

"You didn't go with him? I would have thought you'd want to hang out with your team after a win like that."

Nah, the guys are just having a quiet one downstairs because no one needs the attention right now. I'd much rather sit and talk with—Mia, are you wearing anything under that shirt?"

I looked down and realized the t-shirt was gaping at the neck, giving him a glimpse of the total lack of bra I was sporting. He couldn't see much of my breasts because my weight was on them, but what he could see clearly had all his attention.

"Not a thing," I said, smiling coyly. If he was going to tease me with his body, well, turnabout was fair play.

He let out a heavy breath and glanced to his right, his shoulder moving as though he had adjusted himself.

When he spoke again, his voice was a low rasp that shot straight through my body and made my clit pulse.

"Show me."

I chewed my lip, debating how much I wanted to tease him and weighing it against how appealing the idea of pleasing him was.

Propping my phone up against a set of books on the desk, I moved back until my whole body was visible in the camera frame. Relaxing one shoulder, I let the fabric of my shirt fall down my arm, showcasing my collarbone and a good amount of decolletage.

Oscar licked his lips and sat a little straighter, his gaze intent.

Grinning, I did a little hop to bring the collar of my shirt straight before pulling it down a little further on the other side.

This was my favorite part of burlesque. The tease. Knowing that your audience hung on every inch of exposed skin. The fact that my audience was one person, someone that I was interested in knowing a little better, gave me an even bigger thrill.

Turning my back on him, I crossed my legs and bent at the waist, knowing he would get a glimpse of the curve of my ass and the tiniest hint of the pink flesh between my legs when I did so. Oscar's groan was so loud it seemed to echo around my room, and I straightened, spinning toward him before he could see the way my body was responding to his noises.

"Touch yourself," I urged, lifting the shirt until the hem flirted with the tops of my thighs.

Oscar cursed, and the camera shook for a moment before he settled back down.

"Are you doing it?" I asked and then grinned as he hissed, his head kicking back so that all I could see was the length of his throat.

I turned side-on to the camera and bent my knees, bringing the fabric to my waist so he could see my whole leg and hip.

"Fuck, Mia. You're perfect. The things you do to me…"

"Show me." Old Mia never wanted to see a penis, hell, New Mia hadn't either, but something about Oscar made me feel like a completely different person. Someone who didn't have to hide who she was or what she wanted.

"Are you sure?" Oscar asked, a muscle working in his cheek.

"I had it in my mouth last week, Oscar. I promise I'm not going to go into shock at the sight of your erection."

He barked a laugh, the surprise on his face telling me he hadn't thought through his reservations. And then the camera was moving. Down his hairless chest, two small brown nipples peaked on top of strong pecs and over the stupidly hard, sculpted mounds of his abs. If he weren't the most down-to-earth, humble person I'd ever met, I'd wonder if he was real. Hell, I still wondered if he was a figment of my imagination sometimes.

The camera paused at his lower belly, a fine thatch of light brown curls beneath his wrist. The camera moved as though he were taking a deep breath and then there it was. Long and veined and perfectly in proportion with the hand that stroked lazily up until it covered the deep pink tip and down until his fist settled against his stomach.

"Faster," I muttered, staring intently as he picked up the pace in response to my words.

"Babe, I won't be able to make it last if you keep staring at me like that."

"You're beautiful." The camera shook with Oscar's laughter, followed by a deep groan.

"Mia. Would you dance for me?"

I stepped back as the camera returned to his face. A lovely flush colored his throat and ears, and I wondered if it was arousal or my compliment that put it there.

Turning my back on him, I removed the shirt in one fluid motion and couldn't suppress the grin when I heard a thud and looked over my shoulder to see a view of the ceiling of his hotel room.

Oscar's large hand covered the screen for a moment and then he was back, a playful scowl on his face. "Jesus, Mia. Warn a guy first."

Instead of answering, I started to move my body to a beat only I could hear. I thought about the movements Francesca taught us the week before and followed the basic idea as I moved back and forth in front of the camera. Oscar cursed when I faced him, and I moved closer to give him a good look.

"Don't come yet, I'm still playing."

He cursed again, but his desperate groan told me he would play along.

I ran my hands up the sides of my body, cupping my breasts as I moved my body and marveled at the freedom the screen gave me. No one could touch without my permission. The only person who could see me was who I chose. And he was hanging on to every movement.

My thighs became slick as I teased both Oscar and myself until I thought I would explode. Only then did I move back toward the camera where he waited; his features tight with desire.

"Come for me. Show me what I do to you."

Oscar gasped, and the camera moved down until I could see one hand fisted at the base of his cock as string after string of pearly white cum erupted from his head, painting his lower belly in a mess I wished I could clean up with my tongue. When I told him as much, he groaned, his cock twitching in approval before he brought the camera back up to his face.

"I need to clean up, but I don't know if I can move now."

I grinned, retrieving my shirt and pulling it back over my head. "Well, I'd love to help, but you're a little far away."

He nodded, giving me a sleepy smile.

"Away games suck, but we'll be home tomorrow. Do you want to hang out?"

"Only if we study. I haven't even looked at our assignment for sports psych yet."

Oscar yawned. "It's a date. Cian is spending the weekend at his parents' place so my room's free, if you don't mind coming to the guy's dorm. I promise, we don't live like pigs. I was brought up right."

I chuckled, watching his blinks get longer as his words started to drawl.

"Sounds good. I'll see you tomorrow."

Oscar grunted something unintelligible as a sharp click came through the camera.

"What the fuck, man?"

The phone went flying, my view of the room spinning past a guy's face that was painted in shock and disgust before I was left with a closeup view of a hideous paisley carpet.

Chuckling, I ended the video call, leaving Oscar alone to explain why he was almost asleep with his cock out and cum all over his stomach.

I crawled into bed and brought up the photo of Oscar from the game again.

Maybe this one was safe.

Maybe this one I… liked.

Chapter Eleven

OSCAR

"THEY WOULDN'T BELIEVE me when I told them I was talking to you," I said, grinning despite the embarrassment I still felt as Mia rolled around my bed in hysterics.

"Seriously, Cian asked if I had a porn addiction I hadn't told him about. I've been living with the dude for three years now! Wouldn't he have known that shit before now? Even worse, he told Fraser and he got everyone on the bus calling me Captain Cum."

Mia's face flushed a deeper red as her eyes filled with tears.

"Captain… Captain Cum. Oh my god, I'm gonna pee," she gasped, curling into a ball and holding her stomach as her whole body shook with giggles.

"You could have stayed on the call a minute or two more and been my alibi, you know," I grumbled half-heartedly. If I had to die of embarrassment to make her laugh like this, I'd get creative because I'd never seen her looking so carefree. Her hair was a wild tangle around her head as she sat up, trying to catch her breath around the intermittent giggles that were still bubbling out of her. She sniffed and wiped the back of a hand over her eyes before leveling me with an apologetic look so fake I wanted to tickle her as punishment.

"I shouldn't have let you fall asleep on the phone while you were naked and covered in cum."

"You don't mean that."

"In my defense, you looked cute getting all sleepy and I didn't know you were completely naked at the time."

I shook my head and threw a piece of candy at her.

"Instead of me reliving my traumatic experience again, how about we get some studying done."

Mia groaned and buried her head in my comforter. I'd been trying to ignore how good she looked in my bed, but there was a reason I'd chosen to wear jeans today and they were already coming in handy, even if it meant I was uncomfortable with the tight confines. We hadn't spoken about the implications of what we'd done while I was away, but I thought we were well on our way to dating. I just wasn't sure if Mia was ready to hear it yet or not. It hadn't escaped my notice that she knew a lot more about me than I knew about her. She was an expert at evading questions she didn't want to answer, and while I could respect her desire for secrecy, it was beginning to feel like she was keeping me at arm's length.

"So, aren't Olympic trials coming up soon? Your brother must be excited," I said as casually as I could.

She paused, half off the bed, in her reach for her textbook.

"He doesn't really talk about it much, but he's in the best condition of his life and I know he'll do well."

"What's his event?"

Mia shot me a narrow look as though trying to work out my motivation. She could look all she liked, I was an open book. I wanted to know more about her, and her brother was the only topic she hadn't yet steered away from.

"The two hundred meter butterfly is his favorite event, but there's a few others he competes in," she said eventually, returning her attention to the textbooks she had brought with her.

"Will you go watch him compete?"

"Ahh, I'm not sure. It really depends on what day the trial falls on. I might have to watch it on TV."

"I'd love to watch it with you—"

"What's with all the questions about my brother? He's a cranky bastard who hates everyone but me and would rather grow gills and live at the bottom of the ocean than have to socially interact with literally anyone."

"I'm trying to get to know you, Mia. I feel like I've told you all this stuff and I know nothing about your life."

Mia dropped her eyes to her hands, picking at her nails like they'd committed a felony.

"There's nothing interesting to know. I didn't grow up like you did. End of story."

"Bullshit."

Her face darkened as her eyes flashed up to meet mine, but as fast as her temper flared, she smoothed it over with a smile.

"You're right. You know all kinds of interesting things about me, like how I feel in your arms."

She crawled across the bed and straddled my legs.

"You know how warm my mouth is." Taking my hand, she slid my thumb past her lips, sucking hard until I was cursing the jeans idea. Things were getting painfully tight especially when she dropped her hips and ground herself against my trapped erection.

"Mia," I warned.

Releasing my thumb from her mouth with a pop, she threaded her arms around my neck, tangled her fingers in my hair, and gave it a sharp tug that made me growl.

"Relax, Oscar. Play with me." Her words ghosted over my lips, the space between us all but gone.

I didn't want to play, but I sure as hell wanted her.

She felt like a butterfly. Beautiful, fragile, but evasive, as though a strong enough breeze could carry her so far away I'd never see her again. That possessive part of me roared in denial, and to prove to myself that she was still here, still vital and well, I closed the gap between us.

Her lips opened under mine, and I reveled in the taste of her as I speared my tongue into her mouth, tasting the candy she had just eaten.

Mia continued to rock her hips, but the friction wasn't enough. Wrapping my arms around her, I flipped our positions, putting her beneath me and taking over the rocking. Mia's breath caught, and through the haze of lust, I pulled back to check on her.

"Keep going," she said, pulling at the hem of my shirt. I reached between my shoulder blades, grasped the fabric, and pulled it over my head, then tossed it aside.

The feeling of her eyes on me would never get old. There was a wonder there that I didn't understand. In the past, I'd had bunnies tell me I'm ripped, say absolutely obscene things about what they would like me to do to them, but it was just a body. It functioned the way I wanted it to, and as long as I kept it in good condition, I hoped it always would.

Mia made me feel like I was more.

She dragged her nails over my chest and abs, making me twitch when she hit a ticklish spot, and cupped my cock through my jeans.

"I want you."

My head was pulsing — both of them — but I forced myself to try for some degree of civility.

"Are you sure?"

Mia huffed and worked my button and zipper instead of answering. I caught her hands, forcing her eyes up to mine.

"Seriously. Mia, I want you so bad I can barely breathe, but I need to know you want this even more. If this is to distract me, or you're not one hundred percent certain, we can go back to studying and pretend nothing happened."

Her eyes softened. "I want to have sex with you, Oscar. Is that clear enough?"

Maybe I was being ridiculous. I'd listened when my mom sat me down and taught me about the birds and the bees, and I knew Mia was already showing enthusiastic consent, but I'd had to hear the words. My sisters would be so proud if there were ever a chance in hell I'd talk to them about something like this.

Head in the game, Cavanaugh.

While I'd been thinking about my sisters — what the fuck was wrong with me? — Mia had slid my jeans down my hips, freeing my erection from its confines. Her small hand worked my length, pulling a groan from deep in my chest.

"Fuck, Mia. You're amazing. You're the most beautiful butterfly in the tree."

"I'm what?" she asked, amusement thick in her voice. Instead of trying to explain what the hell I was thinking, I dipped down and pressed my lips to hers.

"Can I see you?"

Immediately, I mourned the loss of her hand, but as she wiggled out of her clothes, I took the opportunity to kick off the bad-idea jeans and retrieve a condom from my bedside table.

She was even more beautiful in real life. Sure, I'd seen her almost naked when she danced, but this was different. Better. She was here with me, and I could touch her and worship her body the way I'd wanted to since I first laid eyes on her.

"I want to make you feel so good," I murmured as she laid beside me.

"No foreplay, I want you now. Just fuck me, Oscar. Please."

"I…Okay, if you're sure." Ripping the condom out of the packet, I rolled it over my length and covered Mia with my body.

"Please, Oscar."

I notched my cock at her entrance and pushed in slowly, a shiver running down my spine as her warmth welcomed me home. Heaven. Bottoming out inside her, I paused to give her a moment to breathe.

"How are you doing?" I asked, dropping a kiss on the tip of her nose.

"Move," she choked out, so I complied. Using long, slow strokes, I angled my hips, dragging the head of my dick along her walls in search of the spot that would make her see stars.

Her eyes grew wide, the silver receding as her pupils blew large. A gasp fell from her lips.

Hell yes, I was going to make it so good for her.

Just as I fell into a rhythm, she braced her hands against my stomach and shoulder, forcing me to stop.

"Like this," she murmured, crawling shakily from beneath me and turning so I was behind her. I couldn't deny the sight of her ass presented to me was a thing of beauty, and I slid back inside her with a strangled moan.

"Are you okay?" I asked.

She pushed back against me and I mentally slapped myself for worrying so much. She'd tell me if something was wrong. Running a hand along her spine, I marveled at the smooth expanse of flesh. She was perfect.

When she grunted, pushing back against me again, I chuckled and fell into a quick rhythm.

I wasn't going to last. The sight of my dick disappearing inside her, coupled with the sounds of our skin slapping together, ramped me up in a way that made my balls pull up and my lower back cramp. I needed to taste her.

On the brink of orgasm, I reached for her chin, guiding her face to mine and froze.

Her expression was a blank mask. Emotionless and dead.

My dick didn't get the memo, erupting in an orgasm that took me out at the knees, even as guilt swamped me.

This hadn't been an intimate moment for Mia.

She hadn't even been here.

The second my dick finished kicking, I withdrew from her heat, tossing the dirty condom in the trash as though it contained toxic waste. What the fuck was wrong with me?

I should have known. Should have been able to stop, for fuck's sake.

Pacing naked in my bedroom, I fisted my hair, like I could tear it from my head.

This was all wrong and I didn't know how to fix it.

"What's wrong?" Mia asked, pulling my comforter up over her, as though she couldn't stand me seeing her vulnerable.

"W-what's wrong?" I laughed, and even I could hear the edge of hysteria in it.

"Who did you just have sex with, Mia?"

She frowned, her fingers tightening on the sheets.

"You?"

"Where did you just go? Because you sure as shit weren't here with me. You didn't even come! Fuck, I get more emotion from my hand."

I paced back toward her and stood at the foot of the bed. She looked so small amongst my sheets, and in that moment, I came to a decision.

"That's not happening again."

Her eyes shone a moment before she dropped her gaze and started searching the bed for her discarded clothes.

"I understand."

"No, I don't think you do. Next time, it'll be all about you and you'll experience every. Damn. Second. You're mine. That means body, mind, and soul, Mia."

Chapter Twelve

Mia

You're mine. That means body, mind, and soul.

Even a week later, thinking about the intensity of Oscar's expression when he said those words gave me chills. My mind was a mess of fear and desire, and I wasn't sure what to do with it all. When I'd initiated things with Oscar, I'd been riding the high of knowing he'd follow my lead. He was a safe person to be with. But the feelings he'd pulled out of me were so intense, so unfamiliar that I couldn't face him. Vulnerability was my greatest fear. God, I wished I could be afraid of birds, or something equally normal, but no. Fucked up Mia was afraid of anyone seeing me. I hadn't lied when I told Oscar I was afraid of people, but it was an easier thing to admit than my aversion to any kind of perceived softness. No one could see me as anything less than a warrior.

Turning around had seemed like a good idea at the time, but the second I couldn't see who I was with my mind turned on me, cannibalizing itself with thoughts of the past. It wasn't the sweet, giant hockey player who would stop on a dime if he thought I was upset. Instead, it was the faceless others. The ones that took what they wanted and to hell with what I thought. I became old Mia again, retreating into my mind and praying for him to finish quickly so I could leave without being hurt.

Instead, I hurt the one person who didn't deserve it. Oscar blamed himself for something he had no control over. I hadn't just let it happen; I'd been a willing and active participant until my trauma reared its stupid, ugly head. Even worse, he hadn't walked out. Hadn't called me names and cut all contact like he should have.

He claimed me.

If I were stronger, I would let him go. Give him space so he could find a normal girl to fall in love with.

God, the thought of Oscar with someone else made me feel like someone had taken a rusted blade to my heart.

A piece of paper landed on my desk, jerking my attention back to the front of the room where Mrs. Murdoch was explaining recent developments in neuropsychology and the impact these studies would have in the future of coaching and athlete cognition. Retrieving the balled up scrap, I carefully smoothed it out to see the words *are U ok?* scrawled in blue ink.

Don't do it, just ignore him. Let him go.

The pep talk fell on deaf ears.

Glancing toward the other side of the room, I found dark green eyes focused intently on me. He wasn't even pretending to listen to the lecture. I pointed toward the front of the room, hoping he'd get the hint and check back in with the lesson. Raising a single brow, he kept focus on me, waiting for a response.

Stupid, stubborn hockey player.

I slid my cell from my pocket and flashed the screen at him before shooting off a text to the tune of, *Of course I'm fine, now pay attention.*

His responding snort was so loud Mrs. Murdoch turned around to find out who was disrupting her class.

"Sorry, Miss," Oscar said, looking and sounding like the innocent schoolboy I couldn't imagine he ever was.

"Focus, Mr. Cavanaugh. Even if you are likely to have a career in the NHL, you still need to pass this class to get your degree."

"Yes, ma'am."

As soon as Mrs. Murdoch turned her back, Oscar winked at me, then bent his head over his lap. A moment later, my phone buzzed with a text.

> Hockey Hero: It's my turn to plan a date. What nights are you working this week?

>> I have the next three nights at the diner, then dancing Sunday night. We'll have to take a rain check.

> Hockey Hero: You're not avoiding me, are you, Balloon Girl?

>> Why would I do that?

> Hockey Hero: **devil emoji**

> Hockey Hero: Monday night. You're mine. Meet me at the rink at 7 PM.

>> I'll think about it.

Hockey Hero: Trouble.

A SMILE PULLED at my lips as I slid my cell back into my pocket. At the front of the room, Mrs. Murdoch finished up the class with a reminder that there was only two weeks until our first assignment was due. I really needed to work on it in my nonexistent time off.

Speaking of time off... I dodged out the door and hurried toward the dorms to get ready for the diner, losing Oscar in the crowd behind me. Was I avoiding him? Maybe a little.

I wouldn't lie and say the idea of being with someone so genuinely good didn't terrify me. Eventually, I would wreck him and have to hold that guilt. Oscar Cavanaugh wasn't someone I'd get over hurting easily.

Bursting into the room I shared with Violet, I barely saw the sequins and glitter I'd forgotten to clean up after I made my new burlesque costume the night before. Although, I did make a quick mental note to vacuum the room because glitter was a nightmare to get out of things, and I'd noticed Violet had started sparkling in the sun.

I didn't think too much about the fact I'd wiped feathers from the list of materials to use on my costumes.

Throwing on my server clothes, I ran out the door with ten minutes to spare, praying that my piece of junk car would start in the increasingly cold weather.

It didn't.

Turning the key over and chanting increasingly desperate pleas elicited nothing more than choked noises from the shitbox.

Cursing, I dropped my head back on the seat. How the hell was I going to get to work?

The answer came a moment later with a tapping on my window. Cranking the glass open, I looked miserably over at the one person that wouldn't leave my thoughts.

"Need a lift?"

I nodded, gathering my bag and closing up my stupid, useless car.

"When was the last time you got that thing serviced? I heard you cranking it, and it didn't sound healthy at all."

"I don't have the money for a service. Shouldn't a car just go?"

Oscar chuckled. "Not indefinitely, no. I have a friend that can help out, if you leave the keys with me."

I climbed into the cab of his truck, shivering in delight as the engine roared to life and pumped warm air over my chilled skin.

"Why would you do that?" I asked, watching his profile as he navigated us out of the parking lot and turned toward town.

"Because I can. I hate the thought of you getting stuck somewhere because I know your stubborn ass wouldn't call for help."

He was right. I wouldn't.

Instead of acknowledging him, I fished the keys out of my bag and dropped them in his center console.

"Aren't you supposed to be at training?"

He shrugged.

"I could hardly leave you there. It's a quick turnaround, anyway. I'll barely miss anything."

"Oscar—"

"Mia, it's fine. I wanted to. Now, stop arguing and tell me what time you finish."

He glanced over, his eyes flicking over my features as though he had a direct line to my thoughts.

"This is what people do for each other when they care. No relationship is fifty-fifty all the time. Today, I might give sixty and you forty. Tomorrow I might only have thirty, but I trust you to give seventy until I'm up again."

Was that what normal people did?

Luca gave me everything he had. Always. I was forced to give what I didn't have growing up. The idea of balance, of choosing to help and giving what you can, was a foreign concept.

For Oscar, I thought I might be willing to try.

"Seven thirty," I said, watching the road while my thoughts raced in circles. "You can pick me up at seven thirty, if you have the time."

He nodded, throwing a smile my way as he pulled up to the curb outside the diner.

"I'll be here."

***

Oscar's truck was idling at the curb at exactly seven twenty-five. The deep rumble brought a smile to my lips, and I ignored Loretta's good-natured teasing as I hurriedly cleared my last couple of tables.

"That boy is going to treat you right, child. Is he as flexible as he looks? Hoo-wee, if I were twenty years younger…"

"Good night, Loretta," I called and waved to the other waitresses on my way out the door.

Oscar jumped out and circled the vehicle, holding my door open for me as I came down the sidewalk.

"Thank you," I said, climbing into the passenger seat and waiting for him to get back in the truck.

"How was work?" he asked, pulling into traffic and steering toward Fox Academy.

"It was good. We had a steady flow of customers but not anything overwhelming. Not so quiet that Loretta had nothing to do but tease me, either."

"Is that the cook?"

I huffed a laugh, thinking about her.

"Yeah. It sounds like she lived a pretty wild life in her youth. Now she just makes up crazy scenarios for the other waitresses and me when she gets bored. She's extremely interested in you at the moment, actually."

Oscar grinned, his teeth flashing white in the dim light of dusk.

"I think I'd like to meet her. She sounds like a lot of fun."

"She is. Completely incorrigible but fun."

We drove in silence for a few minutes before Oscar took a deep breath.

When he didn't immediately speak, I glanced over curiously.

Flicking his eyes toward me and back to the road, he grunted.

"That date we spoke about for next Monday. That's a while away. It's totally cool if you're tired after work, but if not, what are you doing now?"

I shook my head, opening my mouth to tell him no. To say I needed to work on my assignment.

Maybe to admit that I was chickenshit, and the idea of being with him again made me want to break out in hives almost as much as it made me want to strip naked in front of him and ask for everything.

I was a complicated woman.

Instead, I took a deep breath of my own and did something to make my therapist proud.

I did the hard thing.

"I'm free. What did you have in mind?"

"Have you eaten?"

I nodded. Loretta would have been absolutely appalled if I'd left the diner without food in my belly.

"Perfect. Then I've got something fun planned."

He refused to say anything more, but after pulling into the parking lot — and a close call with the resident crow which left Oscar red-faced and me in peals of laughter — we headed toward the ice rink.

"I told you. He has it out for me," Oscar grumbled, glaring back at the crow as he let us into the building.

"Have you always had a fear of birds?" I asked.

"Pretty much. When I was five, I was playing hide and seek with my sisters and hid in an aviary my gran used to have. Elle thought it would be hilarious to lock me in, and Tia agreed. When I went to climb out and found I was trapped, I panicked. Apparently, birds will take offense to loud noises. They lost their shit, flying around, shitting and scratching while I freaked the fuck out, trying to get the feathers off. Mom found me a little while later crouched in a ball at the back of the cage."

He led me to an equipment closet and held his arms wide.

"So there you have it. My sisters traumatized me at five years old, and now even the sight of feathers makes me hyperventilate. Manly, huh?"

I grinned, feeling like I should give him something in return for his story.

Leaning close, I tipped up onto my toes and kissed the bottom of his jaw. His eyebrows rose, and one arm wrapped around my lower back, keeping me steady. He lowered his head and dropped his lips to mine in the ghost of a kiss before groaning and pulling back.

"If I get started now, I won't stop. Come on. We're here for some fun."

The closet was full of skates in different sizes.

"Have you ever skated before?" His eyes were lighter than I'd ever seen them as he picked out a smaller pair and handed them to me.

"I can't say that I have. Is this an excuse to watch me fall on my ass?"

He took my hand, guiding me out to a bench near the rink where he helped me get strapped into my skates before quickly pulling on his own.

"I feel like a giraffe," I said, swaying on the knife-sharp blades as he helped me step onto the ice.

"You'll get the hang of it," he said, skating backward as he guided me further from the safety of the wall.

He was patient, showing me how to place my feet and push off even when I clung to him and almost made us fall.

"You're doing great. If you believe you can do it, you're halfway there."

"And if I believe I'm going to fall on my ass?" I wobbled, my skate running over a rough piece of ice, and Oscar caught me as my feet slid out from underneath me.

His face was so close, his eyes bright with amusement as his warm breath feathered over my lips.

"Self-fulfilling prophecy, baby."

My laugh was airy and very unlike me. How did he keep doing this to me?

"Climb on my back." Pulling me upright, he turned and squatted.

"What?"

Instead of answering, he just waved his arms behind him until I gingerly leaned into him and wrapped my arms around his neck.

As though it were the easiest thing in the world, he straightened, wrapping my legs around his hips, and took off.

I tried not to choke him as I held his shoulders in a death grip, the seats in the stadium zipping past at a dizzying speed.

"Relax, I've got you," he called over his shoulder, turning mid-stride and taking us backward.

"How are you doing this?" I screamed, anxiously watching the wall get closer and closer until he turned in a smooth glide and took us in a different direction.

"Practice."

It took another couple of laps before I began to relax.

The ice was Oscar's second home, and I'd seen him play. He knew what he was doing. More than that, I knew I could trust him to look after me.

"Hold your arms out," Oscar called, gliding around the curve of the rink and settling into a straightaway. Slowly uncurling one hand and wincing at the nail marks I knew would be beneath his shirt, I held out one arm, then the other, gripping his hips tightly between my thighs.

The cool air of the rink flowed over my face and through my hair, our speed causing the fine strands to float around my head. Leaning my head back, I closed my eyes and completely submitted myself to the feeling of flying.

I felt free.

Tears gathered in the corners of my eyes and the feeling swelled in my chest until it escaped in a laugh. Oscar's hands tightened on my knees, but otherwise, he did nothing to change the moment. He just skated.

We moved over the ice for several laps, until I had completely released the pent up emotion I hadn't known I held. Oscar seemed to just know when I'd had enough.

"That was amazing," I gushed, collapsing onto the bench seat.

"I'm glad you liked it."

"How long have you been skating for?"

Oscar's head was bent over my skates, but his ears burned bright red.

"Oscar?"

"Umm… since I was about seven?"

He still wasn't making eye contact, and I got the sense there was a story.

Oscar hadn't batted an eyelid at telling me about his bird phobia, but this made him balk?

Pulling off my skates one at a time, he stole a peek at me, returning his eyes to the skates when he noticed my interest.

Once my feet were free of the skates, he straightened with a sigh, and headed back toward the rink. Three steps out onto the ice, he turned to face me, his face a bright red that made me wonder what could be so bad.

Another deep breath.

When he began to move this time, I couldn't do anything but gape. Instead of the rough and tumble, skirmish skating of hockey, or even the sprints we had just done, his movements flowed like water. Without music, he danced on the ice, easily lifting a leg on a turn before sweeping it forward and jumping into a spin. This was why he had no problems finding a rhythm with dance.

He already knew how to move. After a few more jumps, he came back to the edge of the rink, his eyes on his skates as though he had something to be ashamed of.

"That…"

"That was what happens when you have older sisters who don't like going to activities alone."

"Oscar." I reached up, way up, because he was a giant without skates on. With them, I could barely reach his face.

"That was one of the most beautiful things I've ever seen."

"You think?" The vulnerability in his eyes was something I would normally have run from, but I was learning from this giant teddy-bear of a man that maybe vulnerability wasn't always a weakness. Maybe it was the way to live confidently.

"I loved it. Did you do it with Elle?"

His lips tipped up, and he grasped my hand, pulling me down onto a bench with him as he began to take off his skates.

"Yeah. Elle was always the one forcing me to do things with her. I actually didn't mind the figure skating, though. I was too tall for competition skating, but it's how I found hockey. I guess I should be grateful she was always the bossy sister."

I laughed. "I guess so."

"Siblings. Am I right?" He rolled his eyes with a grin that softened the statement, then picked up both our pairs of skates and left me to put my shoes on.

"Yeah. Siblings," I murmured, wondering what Luca would make of him.

Chapter Thirteen

Mia

AFTER THE THRILL of our skate, Oscar invited me back to his room for ice-cream, warning me that Cian worked late on a Wednesday tending a bar a couple of towns over.

I appreciated the subtle implication that we would be alone in a bedroom setting, but maybe the cold had gone to my head because I felt inclined to trust Oscar with everything.

The thought should have terrified me.

As he let me go first into his space, I noted the differences between my room and his. Not a single thing was out of place in Oscar's room. A couple of sports bags were laid out by the door with what looked like freshly laundered clothing and equipment inside. There wasn't a laundry pile to be seen and both beds had been neatly made.

"Did you guys hire a maid or something?" I asked, noticing the carpet looked freshly vacuumed.

"Nope, this is all us. We made a pact our first year here that we wouldn't live like slobs. It stuck, and ours is the only room on this floor that doesn't stink of sweat and three-day old pizza."

"Nice." I wandered around the space, inspecting the textbooks neatly piled on the desk.

"Is Cian your best friend? You talk about him a bit."

Oscar looked up from a bar fridge beside the desk.

"One of them, yeah. He's my hockey best friend, and then Cam is my childhood best friend."

"That's really cool. I like that you have people close to you."

He laughed. "I've been told I have a knack for collecting stray... What flavor of ice cream do you want?"

The panicked look on his face told me he worried I'd think I was one of those strays.

I mean, I was, but I was okay with that. I let him have his out though, wandering over to inspect what was on offer.

"Definitely the cookie dough," I decided, accepting the small tub and spoon he offered.

We ate in companionable silence, seated comfortably on his bed, and I found my mind wandering to the last time we'd been here.

"I'm sorry," I blurted.

"For what?"

"Last time. You know. I kind of checked out on you and that was totally unfair, so... I'm sorry."

Oscar took my empty tub and spoon and set it aside on the table.

"If you don't want to talk about it, then we can pretend it didn't happen. But if you do, I'm all ears. I know trauma when I see it, Mia. It kills me to think you went through anything that causes that kind of a response, but you don't have to apologize. Okay?"

I nodded, dumbly. Did I want to talk about it? Maybe it would make me feel free, like out on the ice.

Do the hard thing.

Damn it, I was beginning to hate that advice.

"My mom wasn't like yours," I started, folding my hands in my lap and focusing on a small ridge in the edge of my thumbnail.

"She was an alcoholic for as long as I can remember. A nasty drunk who hated to be alone, so we got a lot of 'step dads'." I mimed air quotes around the title, disgust rolling through me at the thought of them.

"Most were violent. Luca took a lot of the beatings for me, which I hated more than when I got them myself. Some were worse."

I couldn't do this. My stomach turned at the memory and I tightened my hands into fists. If he was going to leave me, it was better it be now rather than later when I'd had the chance to ruin him.

Keep going.

"I lost my virginity at twelve to a guy my mom dated for two weeks. When I told Mom, she slapped me and told me I was a lying whore. Luca beat the guy up so bad he went to hospital. There were a few others over the years, but Luca got big early and was able to protect me for the most part. Then there was Brady. I'm… Oscar, I'm not good like you. Bad things happen around me. I don't want them to, but I'm pretty sure I'm cursed. I've been in therapy since I was fifteen when Luca got a part time job to pay for my sessions, and I still don't know if they worked. I'm sorry." My throat was tight, my limbs shaking like I was stuck out in the cold.

"Mia."

I couldn't look at him. What did he think now that he knew how damaged I was?

"Mia, look at me, please. I'm only sorry I didn't get to help Luca beat the shit out of that guy. I think I'd like your brother, by the way, but none of that is your fault. Your mother deserves the same for what she said to you."

I huffed a watery laugh.

"She got worse in the end, trust me."

At his furrowed brow, I shrugged, trying for nonchalance when the thought of that day still kept me up some nights.

"She ran out of alcohol, and Luca flat out refused to get her more. We thought if she detoxed, we could have a real mom. Someone who would love and protect us instead of the vicious, horrible woman that couldn't even leave the house by then. We didn't know alcohol withdrawal could cause seizures. By the time the ambulance came, she was gone."

I looked into his eyes, the deep pools of empathy pulling the last piece of truth from me. The part I hated about myself.

"I was happy when I found out she was gone."

Oscar wrapped me in a hug I felt right down to my blackened soul.

"She was never a mother. I'm so sorry you went through that."

I took his strength. Soaked it into me as though it could mend all my broken pieces and put me back together.

"Oscar? Will you make me forget? I promise I won't leave you this time."

He pulled back, searching my eyes for who knew what, but what he saw must have assured him I meant what I said.

Piling his pillows up, he guided me toward the head of the bed and pulled my shirt over my head before guiding me to the mattress.

"Hold on here. Don't let go, okay?" I took a firm grip on the bed head and watched him slip my jeans off my feet one at a time. When I was in nothing but a bra and panties, he stood back and ran his eyes over my body.

"You are the most beautiful creature I've ever seen. Inside and out. I know you don't see it, but I will make it my mission to help you find it. You deserve good things, Mia Maddren, and if I make you happy, you can guarantee I want to be one of those good things."

Without giving me a chance to answer, he dipped his head and took my mouth in a soul-searing kiss. One hand ghosted up my side in long strokes, then dipped under my bra to tease my nipple. Breaking away from me, he scooped both hands under my bra cups and lifted both breasts out of their fabric enclosure, taking their pink tips into his mouth one at a time. My breath caught as an unfamiliar sensation shot through my body, my lower belly warming as though there was a wire running from my nipples to my pussy.

"Oscar," I breathed, squeezing my knees together to ease the tension.

"Patience. I'll get there." He reached behind my back, unsnapping my bra and sliding the material up until it hung loosely around my wrists.

Moving slowly, he trailed wet kisses down my sternum and my ribs. He stopped, giving me a playful smile as he swirled his tongue in my belly button, blowing a cool breath over it afterward that made my clit pulse.

Pressing small bites over my lower belly, he worked his way down until he placed a kiss over my panties at the top of my mound. Hooking his fingers in my underwear, he slid the fabric down my legs. My breath seized in my throat.

"Oscar, I've never…" My face burned as I tried to find words.

His green eyes flashed up to mine, a darkness there that bordered on violence.

"Well, we're going to fix that. It's a fucking crime that no one has bothered to take care of you before. Relax, baby. I've got you."

I wasn't sure I knew how to orgasm with someone else.

Settling on his elbows between my legs, Oscar looked as though he was getting comfortable.

"Fucking perfect," he whispered reverently, running a thumb up through my folds before he dropped his head and took a long lick. I gasped, my stomach contracting, and I barely managed to keep my hold on the bed as he proceeded to devour my pussy.

No other word could have sufficed to describe the way he ate at me like I was his last meal. I groaned, pushing my pussy into his mouth.

Toys had never felt like this.

He pushed first one, then another finger inside me, dragging them along my inner walls until he found that spot. The one that had freaked me out the first time. Suddenly, I no longer felt in control. Something was building inside of me and I worried that on the other side would be nothing but devastation.

"Oscar." I sounded lost. Vulnerable.

He lifted his head, noting the tone in my voice and gave me a reassuring smile.

"Trust me, babe. You're safe. You can let go."

With that, he went back to his meal and the feeling grew exponentially until I burst.

There was no other way to describe the feeling as a pleasant numbness spread through my body, followed by an overwhelming tide of emotion that drowned me.

The tears weren't just unexpected, they were downright embarrassing.

Nevertheless, after the first and only orgasm I'd ever had that hadn't been self-served, I lay on Oscar's bed, wracked by sobs that wouldn't quit. Wiping his mouth, he crawled up the bed, hauling me into his arms, and lay with me as I cried for everything that was broken in me. Everything outside of my control. Everything I used to be.

As the tears slowed, I became aware of a large palm drawing slow, soothing circles on my back.

"I'm a mess."

"Correction, you're a hot mess."

I hiccupped a laugh and settled deeper into his arms.

"Why do you bother with me? You could literally have any girl you wanted, but you keep putting up with my bullshit."

Oscar sat in silence for a while, his hand moving in a rhythm that made me sleepy.

"I'm not as perfect as you think I am." His soft words broke through my peaceful daze. Holding my breath, I waited to see if he'd go on.

"I had a friend who…my friend Katie came to Fox the same year as me and Cam. Her older sister was Elle's best friend so we became friends by default. She followed us everywhere. We didn't think about it too much at first, Cam had basketball and I had hockey and we just kind of… got busy. Anyway, I had this game one night and when we finished, there was a bunch of voicemails on my cell from her. I'd already organized to head out with the guys for drinks so I ignored them. I figured they'd keep until the morning. Anyway, Cam called me a few hours later to tell me Katie was drunk at a house party and had called him for a lift home. He wanted me to come with him because she sounded off."

He shifted under me, his body tense as he relayed an experience that was obviously distressing.

"You don't need to —"

"No, please. Let me get this out."

His chest rose under my cheek. "It was pissing down rain in the middle of February when we got there, and she was on the roof in a sundress. She lost her shit when she saw me, screaming that she'd always been in love with me, but I'd never seen her. She said it over and over. *Can you see me now?* I didn't know… What was I supposed to say? I thought we were friends who got busy when we got to college. I knew damn well she was sad, but I was so stuck in my own head that I missed exactly how bad things had gotten for her. And then she slipped."

His heart hammered as he said the four little words that finally unlocked the mystery of Oscar Cavanaugh. The hockey player who didn't mess around with puck bunnies. The sweet, charming guy who was honest to a fault. Who had a savior complex a mile long and thought I was someone in need of rescue.

"I'm not Katie," I whispered, scared of disturbing his unloading, but needing to disprove my suspicion before my heart cracked in two.

"No, you're not. But I won't deny the sadness in you was the first thing I noticed."

Chapter Fourteen

OSCAR

THE NEXT FEW weeks were some of the best of my college experience. Mia and I stole moments between her jobs and my training schedules. Once she decided she could trust me with her orgasms, she was insatiable, pulling me into quiet corners, bathrooms, and even once cornering me in the showers after hockey practice. She seemed to revel in taking me to the edge and demanding her own release before I followed her over, and I was happy to let her lead.

We worked together to get our sports psych assignments in, using pleasure as a motivation to run through notes and get words on the page when the call of a new date adventure made it hard to focus. Mia's curiosity and sense of adventure was unlike anyone else I'd met. After our dance class, she suggested doing a day trip up to the mountains, which was great until a fucking eagle decided to crash the party and I heroically hid in the truck while Mia cried with laughter.

It was almost perfect.

While Mia was working at the diner, I took a rare chance to catch up with Cam to shoot some hoops at the outdoor court.

"Have you seen your crow friend recently?" Cam asked, passing the ball and waiting for me to return it to start our one-on-one bout.

"Ha. Ha. You're hilarious," I deadpanned, tossing the ball at his chest and falling back to take up a defensive position.

"All I'm saying is that you spend more time thinking about that bird than you do about Mia."

He popped up and tried for a three pointer. Intercepting the rebound, I dribbled to the edge of the key and took my own shot.

"Only one of them is likely to wear me as a skin suit. It's about threat perception, not affection, jackass."

"You're ridiculous." He laughed, knocking the ball from my hands and executing a perfect layup.

"So, what's the deal with you and Mia's roommate?"

Cam's ears went pink. "No deal. Are you going to pass that off or what?"

I grinned, ready to feed him some of the shit I'd copped when a familiar face passed on the other side of the fence.

Dark hair, squirrelly eyes, and not as big as me by a long shot. Brady was a piece of shit who had made Mia feel like nothing, and he had no business sneaking around my fucking school.

Without thinking, I jogged to the fence, ignoring Cam's curse behind me.

"Hey, Brady, right? What are you doing here?"

The douchebag turned at the sound of his name, squinting in my direction as though trying to place me.

"Do I know you?"

"You will if you don't get gone and leave Mia the hell alone."

He cocked his head, taking a step toward the fence line before he tipped his head back, laughing.

"Ohh, you're the hockey boytoy she's been playing with. I have to say, you were a straight up killer on the ice after you saw me giving it to my girl."

"She's not yours," I growled.

"She'll always be mine. I let her have some space every now and then, but she always comes crawling back." He enunciated the two words like they were something to savor. Something to anticipate and I felt my stomach turn with rage. Over my dead body would he get anywhere near her again.

"Listen, and listen good, fucker. Mia is done with you. If I find you anywhere near her again, I'll kill you myself."

He grunted, his lips curling up into an acerbic smile.

"We'll see, kid."

Cam gripped my shoulder in a bruising grip as the asshat sauntered off.

"Don't do anything stupid, for god's sake."

"I won't if he won't."

***

Balloon Girl: Can you pick me up at 10?

THE SIGHT of the text made my chest swell with pride. Sure, I had to pick her up since I dropped her at the cabaret after our latest date, and her car was sitting in the Fox Academy parking lot, but there was something so domestic about the request. She didn't mind asking for my help, and that made me happier than I could possibly express. I hadn't told her about the run-in with Brady the douche, but seeing as she hadn't brought him up, I figured the job was done. He could wriggle into the night where he belonged and we could live happily ever after. Did I just mentally quote *Ace of Base*? Yes. I was secure enough in my masculinity to use a reference when it was that apt.

Checking my watch, I lifted a hand in farewell to Cian, who barely looked up from his video game as I headed out the door. I had a thought that he was another person I'd neglected lately with the time I was spending with Mia. Doubling back, I leaned back through the door.

"Hey, man. Wanna go for lunch after practice tomorrow?" Cian flicked his eyes up for a second, then refocused on his game, but the corner of his mouth tipped up.

"Like a date? Sure, man, you can take me out."

I snorted and flipped him a bird he didn't see as I headed out to my truck.

Life was good.

Cranking the stereo, along with the heat, I spent the drive wondering what Mia would think of the surprise I had planned. The bed of my truck was piled high with blankets, her favorite ice cream in the cooler… and *The Mask* loaded on my tablet for us to watch under the stars. I'd even packed a couple of hand heaters in case she got cold.

I parked behind the club, thinking of the first time I came here. Foster's twenty-first had sounded like a fun idea because it was something different from the usual 'hit up the bar and pull bunnies' that everyone else chose to celebrate birthdays. I could never have guessed that night would change my life. I was in love with a strong, smart, survivor of a woman who I was pretty sure felt the same way about me.

While I wasn't impulsive enough to come out and tell her how I felt so early in the relationship, I was keen to introduce her to my family and see all my favorite women in one space. Mom had suggested I bring Mia home for Christmas and invite Luca to come too, if his schedule allowed.

The holidays were going to be awesome. After what Mia had told me about Luca, I couldn't wait to see how my sisters handled him.

Pushing through the front door, I felt the music wash over me. It was a pretty cool setup, and I knew exactly where to find Mia, so there was no sense of disorientation like I'd experienced the first time. With sure steps, I crossed behind the setup of chairs, studiously ignoring all the feathers on the costume of the last performer of the night, and headed down the corridor toward the girl's dressing rooms.

Déjà vu hit me like a bolt out of the blue as two shadows, engaged in a heated discussion, became visible, illuminated by the exit sign over the back door. I closed the distance, half expecting Mia to slip out into the night like she had the first time, but this wasn't a memory. Brady the douche gripped her arm, and when she couldn't break his grip easily, I lost my mind.

One moment, I was slowly walking down the hall, and the next I'd tackled Brady through the door and onto the cold ground outside. My fists rose and fell in a tempo that rolled through my shoulders, sending blood flying beneath me.

"Oscar."

"I. Told. You. To. Leave. Her. Alone." I punctuated each word with another hit until soft hands wrapped around my bicep, halting my movements instantly.

"Stop." Her voice was soft, but the defeated tone could have knocked me flat.

"Mia—"

"Not here."

She turned and walked off without a second glance at the guy I left bleeding in the dirt.

Chasing her down, I thought better of grabbing her, settling for trotting alongside her until she reached my truck and waited for me to unlock the door.

We drove in silence, sadness wafting off her in waves that broke my heart, even as I struggled to wrap my head around what had happened.

It wasn't until I'd pulled into a parking spot at Fox and killed the engine that I turned to her, hating the blank mask she wore.

"I'm sorry."

A tear tracked down her cheek, and I was powerless to resist reaching for it. The touch of my skin against hers seemed to be what broke the spell.

"I told you that I'm not Katie," she said, her voice so low that I flinched.

"I know—"

"I'm still talking. You think you're some wounded hero that can ride in and fix my life? It was fucked up a long time before I met you and I. Fixed. It. Me. I don't need you to try to save me, especially when you're destroying your own life to do it."

I opened my mouth, but she held up a hand.

"How many times have you been penalized for being late to practice because you were helping me? I'm grateful, I am, but what happens if Brady presses charges? You think I want your lost NHL career on my conscience? Don't you dare put that on me. I'm not Katie. I'm just Mia. I'm enough for me. I don't know if I'm enough for you, but that's a you problem. Please don't follow me. I think we're done here."

# Chapter Fifteen

*O*SCAR

"H*E'S STILL MOPING*?"

"Yup."

"Have you tried turning him off and on?"

"I mean… I kicked him a time or two. I think he's broken."

"Nah, he probably just did something stupid."

"You'd know best, you've known him longer."

"Definitely something stupid."

"Are you two done?" I asked, glaring over at my two supposedly best friends.

"Not even nearly, my man. You've done nothing but lie here and mope for a week now. You didn't even come out on our date. It's time to pull it together. Your game is suffering and Coach has just about had enough."

After Mia put me in my place for being the jackass I was, I'd moved through the rest of the night and the following day in a fog. She'd been right; I was casting her as a version of Katie I could save, even if I hadn't been conscious of it. The problem was, that reasoning didn't explain why I felt so miserable after effectively doing the 'saving'.

My sheets still smelled like her.

On Tuesday, I'd had to sit in sports psychology knowing where she was in the room, but I couldn't get her attention. I'd broken her trust and fucked up the good thing we had.

"Come on, big guy. It's time to stop being a sad sack and come up with a game plan." Cam came over and pulled at my arm until I reluctantly sat up.

Huh. I was wearing the same clothes I'd put on Tuesday morning.

Cam flopped on my left and Cian took up my right as they waited for me to formulate some kind of suggestion.

"I don't know what I'm doing here, guys. I thought I was in love with her, but maybe I was being a dick with a savior complex."

"Oh, you definitely were."

I shot a glare at Cian who grinned unrepentantly. "But that doesn't mean you didn't love her. The two aren't mutually exclusive. I think what you need to decide is if it's worth exploring the relationship without being the hero she doesn't need."

I scrubbed my hands over my face, and when I didn't feel any clearer, I grabbed my water bottle off the nightstand and took a healthy drink.

"You need to remind her why she liked you in the first place. Get creative. Everyone loves a big gesture."

"You want to watch me make a fool of myself, don't you?"

Cian snorted. "Oh, absolutely. But I also want my friend back. You're better when you're with her. Don't let her go because you had your first fight."

He was right. Hauling myself off the bed, I shuffled toward the closet and got my shit together.

"What are you going to do?" Cam asked.

"Well… First, I'm going to take a shower."

"And then?" Cam pushed as Cian snorted.

"I'm going to get my girl back."

***

After I was clean and feeling a little more human, I discussed my plan with the guys, leaving Cian in charge of logistics.

This will work.

I repeated my mantra on my way out of the men's dorm, around the building and all the way to the foot of the girl's dorm. Which was when I looked up and lost my shit. Mia was sitting on the edge of the roof, four floors from the ground. From this angle, I couldn't make out her expression, but she was *on the roof*. I threw myself at the entry to the dorms, bolting past open rooms and girls in the hall who looked at me like an escaped zoo animal.

It took no time at all to find the stairwell leading to the roof.

So. Many. Stairs.

My heart was pounding, my breath really short as I hit the final landing and came out onto the roof. Dang, I needed more stair cardio in my future, because that was a workout.

Moving slowly toward the corner I'd seen Mia on so as not to startle her, I let out a very masculine squeak as I was confronted with a new problem.

A soft ruffle alerted me to his presence. Those midnight black feathers moving in a way reminiscent of a rattler about to strike.

The fucking crow was here.

He opened his beak, displaying his creepy bird tongue and croaked, probably telling me how I would die, before it hopped a couple of steps closer.

"Fuck off," I whispered, taking a small step back to keep the distance between us.

It cocked its head, its beady eyeball staring right into my soul and croaked a second time.

"Wait… are you tattling on me?" It occurred to me that this evil beast was making noise. Probably encouraging Mia to do something stupid.

Mia.

With renewed courage, I took a step toward the corner of the roof and the fucking thing took flight in a flurry of feathers and nightmare.

I shouted in what I would love to say was anger, instead of outright terror, and shielded my head from the freaky thing.

"Oscar?"

She looked even sadder than last time I'd seen her, if that was possible. Her face was pale, her eyes dull, and it occurred to me this separation was no good for either of us.

"Hey."

Her lips quirked at the corner as she took a step closer.

"You braved a confrontation with the crow to tell me 'hey'?"

"Evil fucking thing," I grumbled, giving her a reluctant smile.

"I'm pretty sure I saw him researching how to skin a human at the library the other day."

I shuddered. "Don't joke about that shit. I'm scared no one will be able to tell when it's a crow walking around in my Oscar skin."

A giggle burst from her lips, and even though it was my very legitimate and not at all juvenile fear, I was glad to see her smiling.

"I saw you on the roof," I said, waving my hand vaguely toward where she had been sitting.

"It's my quiet place. I come here to think sometimes."

Completely normal and not at all worrisome.

"I didn't know that."

She glanced back at the edge of the roof.

"It's where I do my best thinking."

"Was it working today?"

Her silver eyes flashed back up to mine, a certain something hidden in their depths I couldn't quite read.

"Yeah, I think it was." She cleared her throat.

"So, what brings you to my little corner of the academy?"

I rubbed a palm over the back of my neck, trying to find the right words to show her I understood how much of a fuckup I'd been.

"Remember when I told you about Katie?" Why the hell was I starting an apology with a contributing factor of the conflict? I wanted to kick myself, but instead I doubled down hoping she'd let me make my point before telling me I was an idiot she never wanted to see again.

For a second time.

"I never noticed Katie. She was a friend, and that's all I ever saw her as. I hate to admit it, but I was self-centered. I didn't *see* her. I see you, Mia. Every part of you. I might have got caught up in what I thought you needed me to be — something I promise I'll try hard not to do again — but who you are at your deepest level… I see you."

How many times had I used the word see? Did I even make any sense? Mia was so quiet in the wake of my attempted apology I wondered if I should just leave it. Move schools, change my name, and disappear off the face of the…

"I see you too, Oscar." Her arms wrapped around my neck, and I breathed a sigh of relief as her body melted into mine. Blueberries filled my nose and I wondered if she'd started using a new shampoo. I liked it. Then again, I liked everything about Mia.

"Fuck, I missed you so much," I whispered into her neck.

"It's been five days, Oscar."

"It felt like a lifetime."

She grunted, pulling back slightly. I didn't want to let her go.

"I have something I should tell you, too."

She hadn't seen my grand gesture. Panic flooded me at the thought she might say thanks but no thanks before I had the chance to show her I was the right person for her.

"Hold that thought. I have a surprise for you."

Her eyebrows pulled down, her mouth screwing into a bemused smile.

"O-kay…"

"Can you meet me at the ice rink in an hour?"

"Oscar—"

"Please."

She looked deep into my eyes, trying to read me in a way only she seemed able to. I wasn't giving anything away, though. Part of the value of a grand gesture was the element of surprise.

"I'll be there," she said eventually.

"Good."

Chapter Sixteen

MIA

THE PARKING LOT was quiet as I made my way to the ice rink an hour later as per my invitation. After our short conversation on the roof, I still wasn't sure if I felt better or worse about how we'd left things. Could I trust him to keep his promise?

Before he'd turned up and confronted his archnemesis on my rooftop, I had been musing deeply on our relationship. Since the moment I climbed out of his truck, I'd wondered if I'd done the right thing calling him out the way I did. He had been acting on instinct. That chivalrous part of him that was selfless to a fault had seen Brady as a threat and had jumped to my rescue, but I knew it was a behavior I couldn't encourage. He truly would ruin his life if it meant protecting someone he cared for, and I refused to let him do it for me. I kept circling back to one unassailable conclusion about why I couldn't let Oscar burn his life to the ground.

I loved him.

His intelligence, his honesty, and goofiness, hell, even his fear of birds. All of it drew me in because he was more than his crazy hot body. He meant safety to me.

Since Oscar had refused to let me get a word in edgewise during his apology, I'd decided that regardless of how whatever-this-was went, I was going to tell him how I felt.

Today.

Oscar's roommate met me by the doors, a smirk on his face as he waved me inside.

"Blink twice if you need me to create a diversion, all right?" he murmured as he led me to the edge of the rink.

"I'm not wearing skates," I said, eyeing the ice as though it would bite me. Without Oscar to steady me, I worried it just might.

"Your chariot, m'lady," a tall redhead said, skating over with a chair in front of him.

"Easy, Fraser, you don't want to spill Mia onto the ice and piss off the caveman."

I looked between the guys, unsure what was happening, but with their guidance, I got seated in the chair and allowed Fraser to push me into the center of the ice.

"Are you okay here? The others will be out in a minute, so if there's any problems, just flag us and someone will get you back to dry land. Cav-man is our brother and now you're family, too."

"Shut up, idiot." Cian had strapped on his skates during my journey to the center of the rink and zoomed past us, clipping Fraser over the head on the way through. I grinned, enjoying the easy camaraderie the boys seemed to have together.

I found myself hoping Luca had something similar with the other swimmers on his team.

If I learned nothing else from Oscar, it was the value in true connection with others. He lived and breathed it, his love like an endless pool that anyone would be lucky to drink from.

Other people began to enter the rink, skating in lazy circles, and coming to a stop around me. Each one had a kind smile for me. I realized that whatever he had planned, his whole team had shown up to support him.

"You're not ready for this, but enjoy. Remember, blink twice and I'll get you out."

Cian's wink told me he was kidding, and with a quick squeeze of my shoulder, he skated a little way away and waved at a point way back in the stands.

A very familiar roll of bongo drums preceded brassy trumpets that blared through the stadium speakers, and the big bodies around me began to shift, laughter rippling through the ranks as they tracked something on the ice behind us. The scrape of skates drew closer and just as Jim Carey began to sing about the rumba beat, Oscar came into view covered in… balloons?

Holy shit, he was doing my routine.

Okay, so routine might have been an overstatement.

Bright strings of yarn crisscrossed his body with balloons tied at intervals, enough that most of his torso and hips were covered with the bright latex.

A wolf-whistle sounded close to my ear and I laughed as Oscar turned and shook his ass at his teammate before skating up to him and offering him a small pin. The guy popped a red balloon near Oscar's shoulder before handing the pin back. One by one, Oscar invited his teammates to pop his balloons, executing outrageous moves in between each pop. I wondered if the guys knew Oscar had been a figure skater, because despite the fun and levity of the performance, his skill and grace was still obvious to me. When all the balloons were popped around his torso, he shimmied out of the yarn, handing it off to Cian seamlessly before the guys attacked the balloons lower around his hips.

There was raucous laughter as the balloon covering his ass was popped by Fraser and a very small thong was revealed beneath.

I didn't think I had ever laughed as hard as I did during Oscar's performance, but when he was down to one balloon, everything seemed to slow as he skated slowly toward me.

Offering the pin to me, he leaned in with a conspiratorial wink. "You're the only one I trust to get this close to my dick, Balloon Girl."

I snorted. "Was that a line, Cavanaugh?"

He waved a hand at me. "Nah, not me. I'm too serious for shit like that."

My cheeks ached from grinning as I reached out and placed a gentle slit in the final balloon, letting it deflate slowly as the song wound down.

"That was something else."

"You're something else."

Crouching before me in nothing but skates and a thong, Oscar Cavanaugh was the realest person I'd ever known.

"Mia…"

"I love you," I blurted, cutting off Oscar's speech before it began. His teammates tittered around him, and I remembered Luca telling me that athletes were the worst kind of gossips.

"Clear out, you guys," Oscar said without breaking eye contact with me.

Despite several deep grumbles and accusations of Oscar being a spoilsport, the ice cleared quickly.

"Sorry, I wanted to let you speak, but if I didn't say it, I was going to burst."

"Say it again."

Large hands cupped my cheeks as his bright green eyes burned into me. This man was clearly loved by everyone who came into contact with him; I could understand why because I was right there with them, but he still looked at me like hearing it from me was more important than anything else in the world. He had to be freezing his nuts off out on this ice, but he didn't move, just waited patiently for me to repeat myself.

Taking a centering breath, I looked him dead in the eye so there couldn't be any misunderstanding.

"Oscar Cavanaugh, I. Love. You. I don't know if I had a choice in the matter. You are the most lovable person in the world, and for some crazy reason, you want me. Who am I to tell you no when you make me feel things I didn't think were real, let alone things I could have."

Anything else I might have said was lost as Oscar's lips crashed against mine, his tongue spearing into my mouth as though he could taste the emotion behind my words.

He swept me into his arms, wrapping my legs around his hips and skated us over to the edge of the ice. Despite the chill in the air, something distinctly warm, and not at all shrunken, hardened between us.

"Literally no way of hiding it in this outfit," Oscar grumbled, adjusting himself one-handed.

I grinned, rubbing myself against him like a cat and loving the groan that rumbled out of his throat.

"Fuck, I love you, Mia."

"I know," I said, continuing to move my hips as I trailed kisses down his neck.

His grip tightened on me.

"Are you going to fuck me in those knife shoes?"

"Knife…? Yes. Yes, I think I am. But first…"

He lowered me carefully to my feet and instructed me to get naked.

"Is anyone still here?"

He shrugged. "Maybe. Scream extra loud, just in case."

I gasped, but couldn't deny how my panties dampened at his words. Despite his nonchalant attitude, I knew damn well he wouldn't let anyone see me. It didn't stop the thrill that coursed through me, though.

I lifted my sweater off slowly, waiting for the moment he realized I hadn't bothered with a bra.

The noise he made was barely human, and I found my progress unbuttoning my jeans hampered as Oscar crouched low and buried his head in my cleavage. Cupping my breasts in his big hands, he licked and bit until the flesh was blushed pink from his stubble.

When he was satisfied with the color, he slipped his hands down the front of my jeans.

"Let me help you with these."

Instead of moving them, he cupped my mound, his eyes shooting to mine when he discovered how wet he'd made me.

With a curse, he wrapped a hand around my back and pulled me into a passionate kiss as his fingers continued to play in the mess between my legs. Pushing first one, then another finger inside of me, he swallowed my whimpers as he worked my body right up to the edge before he pulled his hand free and ordered me to drop my pants and spread out on the stadium steps.

The air was chilly on my skin, and as I followed Oscar's instructions and bared myself to him, I felt like a goddess. He towered over my naked body in nothing but skates and a thong, and the adoration pouring off him made me squirm in anticipation.

Ensuring my eyes were on him, he slowly lifted the hand that had been in my pants and ran his tongue along each finger, lapping up my essence like it was honey.

"Delicious," he growled, dropping to his knees before me and forcing my legs wider to get a better view.

"This is the prettiest pussy I've ever seen." He ran a finger through my folds, pausing at my entrance.

"I'm going to eat it until they can hear your screams in the locker room."

My hips lifted in an unconscious invitation. I swallowed a whine, desperate to be filled by him in any way I could.

Reaching over my body, he placed his fingertip on my lips.

"Suck, baby. Show me what you want to do to my cock."

I could taste myself on his finger. As I sucked hard on the digit, swirling my tongue around the tip, I hoped he would take pity on me and give me access to something bigger to suck on soon.

"Good girl," he said softly, pulling out of my mouth with a pop.

"Oscar."

"Shhh." Tracing a line down my throat, he drew a wet circle around each nipple.

"Use your hands to take care of these," he urged, showing me how he wanted me to squeeze and pluck at the reddened tips. My body was a livewire, and every touch sent zaps of pleasure directly to my clit.

Just when I thought I couldn't bear another moment without his touch, he bent his head and licked a long line up my center.

"Oscar!" I kicked my head back, ignoring the discomfort of the cement stairs as he flattened his tongue and worked my pussy with firm strokes.

He hummed, the vibrations making me shiver in delight as he speared his tongue inside me.

"You taste so fucking good, are you getting close, Mia? I want to hear you."

"Yes," I gasped, pushing my hips harder onto his tongue and chasing the sensations I needed to get me there.

"Come on, baby. It's time to give me your first orgasm for tonight. It's been too long."

Lashing my clit with his tongue, he plunged two fingers inside me and crooked them in just the right way.

I screamed, my voice becoming hoarse as the intensity of the orgasm hit me hard. My body shook, and Oscar wrapped me in his arms to avoid bruising the crap out of my back.

As my shudders subsided, Oscar slid his thong off over his skates and paused.

"I don't have a condom."

"The one downside of your costume is the total lack of pockets," I joked.

He snickered. "I don't know how you girls do it."

We fell silent, both smiling at the ridiculousness of the moment.

"Oscar, I have an implant."

"A what?" The most adorable look of confusion passed over his face.

"An implant. It's a contraceptive thing. We could… you know. If we're both clean, then it's actually more effective than a condom."

"You would trust me with something like that? I mean, I've never been with anyone bare before, but that's still a lot of trust. Are you sure?"

"Of you? Yeah. I'm really sure."

His boyish grin split my heart open, and a laugh of pure joy bubbled out of my throat as he pulled me into his arms, standing easily with our combined weight.

With a half turn, he pressed my back into the boards and notched his dick at my entrance.

"Are you sure you're sure?" he asked, pressing his forehead into mine.

"Positive. Fuck me on your knife shoes. Just, please don't break an ankle."

His grin turned wicked. "Haven't you heard?" He pushed into me in one long stroke until he was fully seated inside of me.

"I'm multi-talented." Hitching my legs tighter around his waist, his hips snapped into me in increasingly powerful thrusts while his mouth traced wet kisses along my throat.

"Oscar," I mewled, feeling my body tighten around him.

"It's ok, baby. Let go. I've got you."

I put my trust fully in the man holding me body and soul. My vision whitened as sparks flew through my nerve endings, flooding me with a warm sense of love and security. Oscar's thrusts slowed as my hearing came back online, and he grasped me tight, coming with a trembling growl.

"Fuck. Mia. Fuck, you're so beautiful when you come."

He dropped his head into the curve of my shoulder, sucking in deep breaths as he recovered.

"Babe, that was…"

"Risky. Did you check if there were cameras in here?"

He let me slide down his body, waiting for me to find my clothes before he picked his way over to a seat and began unlacing his skates.

I pulled my sweater over my head, then shimmied into my jeans, leaving my panties out to give to Oscar. When I placed the fabric in his hand, he glanced at me, brow furrowed in confusion.

"Those are for you. Now, let's get you presentable enough to go out in public for the walk back to your dorm so we can do that again. Five days was a long time."

He jumped up, kissing me hard and racing to the stairs before backtracking for his thong.

"Don't want Coach finding that. There's no universe where the guys wouldn't throw me under the bus for it."

I chuckled, easily able to see it playing out after spending a little time with his team.

"They love you."

He smiled, throwing an easy arm around my shoulders and steering me toward the locker room.

"I never got a biological brother, so I found chosen brothers in Cam and then in my team. I know they have my back, and I have theirs. Unless it makes a good story."

My laugh echoed off the walls of the stadium as we went to find clothes for Oscar that I could take off as soon as we got home.

THANK you so much for reading!

That's it for Oscar and Mia for now, but you will see them again in Luca's book, Stretch, coming soon in the Perfect Stroke Series.

Want to start the series now? You can read Kane and Darcy's prequel, Split here

SIGN up for TL's newsletter to find out about new books!

WELCOME TO FOX ACADEMY!

Fox Academy

To read more sports romance stories, check out the books below…

Kicking it with the Figure Skater

By Victoria Gillilan

Kicking it with the Swim Captain

by Angelica Kate

Kicking it with the Point Guard

by Emmy Dee

Kicking it with the Tight End

by Faolan Kurayami

To read the Student-Teacher Romance stories that also take place in Fox Academy, check out the books below:

Falling for my Algebra Teacher

by Foxy Valentine

Falling for my Agriculture Teacher

by Linda Marie Pankow

Falling for my History Teacher

By Haven Beck

ALSO BY TL HAMILTON

Moon Dust Library/ Silver Springs Library Standalones

Moonlit Alexandrite

Moonlit Alexandrite: Crafty Seductions

Jewels Cafe: Jacinth

ABOUT THE AUTHOR

Hi guys, I'm TL

I live in Melbourne, Australia, with my hubby, two little boys, Arlo the wonderful, and Hugo the turtle.

I love stories, and daydreaming about new stories, which is why I write all over the romance spectrum from romcom right through to the dark, gritty hold onto your seats drama.

I am happiest when the characters in my head are behaving.

Reviews are the life blood of indie authors, so if you read my work and enjoy it, please consider leaving a review in exchange for my everlasting adoration.

Come and join the fun in my reader group on Facebook

ACKNOWLEDGMENTS

If you've made it this far, my first acknowledgment is to you, the reader.

Thank you so much for coming on another fictional journey with me. Your support is what lets me continue creating these characters I love so much (and I hope you do too!)

To my advanced reader team, thank you again for taking the time to give feedback and spread the word on my latest vivid daydream. A special mention must go to Jamie, my amazing alpha reader who is always the first to see the messy accumulation of ideas that is my first draft.

Zainab, you are the best. You have an amazing way of taking my words and polishing them until they gleam and I appreciate you for being there with a snarky comment and a willingness to claim every MMC I dream up.

To my family and friends, who patiently listen to every new idea and crazy concept I announce and encourage me to keep going when the writing isn't as easy, thank you. I couldn't do this without your support.

Special mention to my author friends, you know who you are, you guys are amazing and between animal memes, GIF conversations, and empathy over muse issues, it isn't an exaggeration to say none of my books would happen without your support.

A huge thank you to Stella from Stellar Graphics for my stunning cover, and a final thank you to Quell for organizing this shared world.

I hope I'll see you all next book and until then, happy reading!